Crash & Burn

The Hells Disciples MC

MC

2

Jaci J.

Crash & Burn © 2014 Jaci J.

All Rights Reserved.

This book is a work of fiction and any resemblance to any person or persons, living or dead, any place, event, occurrence, or incident is purely coincidental. The characters and story lines are created and thought up from the author's imagination or are used fictitiously.

Cover art; Cover done by Margreet Asselbergs of RfR Designs

Cover photos; Big Stock Photos Tumad (45056344) Astor63 (17963390)

This one is for my mom.

No matter what crazy, stupid, or outrageous thing I do, you still love me.

Thank you for your unconditional love, support, encouragement,

*and for **always** having my back and best interest at heart.*

I love you!

A big thank you to the best editor and my crazy kind of manager DANA HOOK. You fucking rock!! Without your help I'd still be floating around in Amazon with a good, but terribly edited and formatted book. You're my favorite book bitch & I thank fuck for all your wonderful help!!

Thank you!!

Again a huge thank you to my best friend and biker mouthed little sister. You're opinion and support has helped me through this crazy adventure. You are the best!! I love you!!

A shout out to Margreet Asselbergs of RfR Design for designing beautiful covers for me. Before you I had an alright cover and now I have perfection. You took my ideas and made them into something amazingly wonderful! Thank you!

To my amazing Beta readers, Chris Alderson Kovacich and Sam Price. Your love of this story and your honest feedback is like gold to me. Thank you for helping and believing in me.

And to everyone who read the first book and loved it, this one is for you!! You're encouraging words and love keep me writing!!

Thank you! Thank you! Thank you!

Play list

1. "Smoke, Drink, Break-up" – Mila J.

2. "Litost" & "Down With Me" – X Ambassadors

3. "Ashley" – Big Sean

4. "Shameless" – Garth Brooks

5. "Tuesday's Gone" - Lynyard Skynyrd

6. "Numb" – August Alsina

7. "High for This", "Valerie", "The Birds (part 2)" – The Weeknd

8. "Poetic Justice" – Kendrick Lamar

9. "Superman" – Eminem

10. "Alive" – Ayah Marar

11. "She Knows" – J. Cole

12. "Go Deep" – Ty Dolla $ign

13. "Waiting Game" – Banks

14. "Holy Grail" – Jay Z

15. "Just Like A Pill" – Pink

16. "Tears in Heaven" – Eric Clapton

17. "Give Me One Reason" – Tracy Chapman

18. "100" – Iggy Azalea

19. "Who Do You Love" – YG

20. "Tiny Dancer" – Elton John

Table of Contents

Since that night there has been no hope, no light. I've been living

in complete darkness ... HELL.

1
Hate

Tank

    Her back has always been tanned, smooth, and so fucking perfect that you can't help but want to touch it, kiss it. I could spend my entire day licking every fucking inch of it because I love her body, her skin. Now as I look at her, I can barely hold back the angry outburst fighting its way from my fucking gut. This shit eats away at me every second of every fucking day. It's all I can see anymore, and I can't stand even looking at her because of it. All I feel is absolute rage at what I see. I stare at those three round, raised, pink scars that mark that perfect skin, and the sight of them make me sick to my stomach. I hate myself for letting it happen to her, and I hate her for looking past it. I hate that she still loves me, and I really hate that I don't deserve it.

Lying in bed together, just after fucking her hard, I can only think of those three goddamn scars. She's lying on her side with her sexy, long ass leg thrown out to the side, giving me another perfect body part of hers that's stained with the reminder of my failure. I've let her down so many times, but that last time will forever be what will take her away from me, whether she wants to see it or not. How can I love her when every time I look at her, I feel disgust for her, for staying here and not leaving me. I want her to see that I did this to her and have her hate me for it, but she still stays 'cause she loves me, no matter how bad I treat her.

It all started happening a few weeks after that night. Things seemed calm enough and we were all tryin' to get back to normal, but then I got a gut check. Maybe it was from all that adrenaline still running through my body 'cause just when I thought I could start to calm down from it all, out of nowhere, it just felt like a ton of bricks were crushing me. I was lying there with Lil in my arms, sleeping peacefully when the nightmare started flashing before my eyes. My body went cold and I started to shake because I was there, and I could feel every fucking emotion I felt that night like it was happening all over again. It didn't matter that she was right here; whole, alive and in my arms. The nightmare felt like it was reality again. All I could do was lay there, freaking the fuck out while clinging to Lil like a life raft.

She's running to me with so much desperation as those shots ring out. I'm not there in time, but I see every jerk of her body as each bullet tears into her. Her eyes go wide with shock as each jerk gets her closer to me, 'cause she doesn't stop running for a second. My baby was hurt, but she has always been so fucking strong. I finally get to her as she runs right into me, knocking us both to the ground. I'm scared shitless 'cause I know she took all three hits. Her breath is ragged and her total stillness consumes me. All I feel is panicked and desperate 'cause I know this shit is bad. It's so goddamn bad.

She's choking now and gasping for air as I flip her off me. There is so much blood covering her. I can smell it and see her fucking struggling to stay alive, all the while staring at me. I can't fucking save her.

Even though I know the outcome, I can't stop the feeling of dread that settles over me like a thick blanket, thinking of her not making it. The image of her body not moving, her eyes dead of life while they are still looking straight at me … she's gone. This time no one saves her and I always wake up in a fuckin' panic, shaking and needing a drink. Drinking and fucking her are the only things that bring me back from the goddamn nightmares.

After six months of this shit, my mind is in a constant state of pissed off and scared shitless. I can have them every night for a week, and then I won't have them for a few days. I might have them as soon as my ass falls asleep, or it could be right before I wake up. I never know when to expect them, and the not knowing is just about as bad as the dreams themselves. The dreams fuck with me. They fuck with us.

I'm constantly worried something is gonna happen to her if she's not in my sight. I always have to know she's alright 'cause it's the only way I can function anymore. The dreams fuel these psychotic feelings and keep my nerves on edge. I feel bad for acting like a fucking nut case whenever she's not around me. I pressure the fuck out of her by blowing up her phone, showing up wherever she's at and wanting to know when she'll be back. I throw all my shit on her. The dreams, the scary as fuck thought that she'll die, and the guilt are eating me alive and I put that shit on her.

****

It's three in the morning and I can't fucking sleep. I sit here, nursing my Jack and smoking my blunt as I stare aimlessly at my beautiful girl. Inhaling the smoke, I fill my lungs as I stare and think. These last few months I've resorted to drinking ... a lot. It's like something won't let me forget. I sit here and try to understand why my mind can't come to terms with the fact she's here, alive and breathing every fucking day. I feel nothing but guilt for not being there, not getting to her in time. My mind is telling me that she may be here, but I fucked up and almost lost her. This bitch has been the stronger of us, and in some way it pisses me off. She's her own savior, I'm her fucking failure.

She forgives me for all of it. She can't understand why I blame myself and that she loves me unconditionally. No matter what I say or do, she's right by my side, always putting up with my shit. After that night, I expected to lose *my* Lil. After what she'd been through, I was sure she'd change. Hell, I wouldn't blame her if she couldn't move on from it and I was ready to be her rock, whatever she needed me to be. I was sure I'd lose the carefree, crazy girl I loved so fuckin' much. That was what I was expecting.

Not a goddamn thing about Lil has changed. If anything, she lives life harder. She's always dancing, singing, smiling for no damn reason at all. She loves me harder, wants me more. She's still everything to me and she's still the reason I do everything I do. That night didn't change her, it changed me. Because of my nightmares, I've become hers.

More recently, I drink, smoke, and stay at the club, hoping to numb the obsessive need for her and the life she should have without me. I want her, yet I want to forget her and feel normal again. No matter how much I hate myself, I'll never be able to let her go. There are a fuck of a lot of clinical words for it, shit like co-dependent, or self-deprecating. In the end, it's just fucking sad. I can't get enough of her, but it kills me just to look at her. I hate her for wanting her so goddamn bad.

****

"How much bacon are you gonna make baby, 'cause it looks like you cooked the entire farm?" Her soft hands push up under the front of my shirt and as I'm standing there at the stove, she leans herself into me. Her warm body against mine always makes me hard. I fight the shiver her touch brings to my skin and fight the need to push her against the counter and fuck her to remind myself that she's mine. These thoughts make me want to drink. She moves her face around my shoulder so I can see that sexy smile and those beautiful eyes as she makes a grab for the bacon. I hate and love the way she looks at me, like I'm the only motherfucker she wants. Shit makes me feel guilty as she damn near dances away from me into the living room.

I moved her stuff into my place right after she got out of the hospital. I needed her close where I could always find her. I thought having her here would help and it does, but not the way I'd hoped. How do you love someone so fucking much, and want to hurt them all the time? She changed a few things around my place. Thought it'd bother me, but it doesn't. It just reminds me she's here with me right where I want her, but I feel like shit for wanting it that way.

"You goin' to the club today?" she asks from the couch a few minutes later. There's a touch of uncertainty when she asks me. It's a tone she uses a lot with me now; always careful about what she says around me. She shouldn't have to hold shit in, but I shouldn't make her feel like she has to, either. She's surrounded by school books, her computer propped up on her lap, those cute ass glasses on her nose. She's so beautiful it hurts to look at her and I'll never truly understand how I got so goddamn lucky.

"Yeah. No need to wait up, I may be late again."

Her eyes lose some spark and that smile slips ever so slightly, but she nods anyway. My fucking little soldier holding that shit down for me, because I'm a fucking asshole and can't take it. Not enough sleep is giving me a real fucked up attitude. I decided to try and soften the blow, so I got up and started making her breakfast, thinking it could make her day a little easier to deal with me.

"Me, Peaches, n' Lailah are goin' into town to look at cars. Do you wanna come?" she asks, lacking any confidence. I catch the name Lailah. She's no one I know and yet I don't give a fuck enough to ask. She knows my answer to her question before she asks, but she loves me, so she asks anyway.

Shaking my head I mutter, "Can't. Got too much shit to do. "

She gives me a half-hearted smile and nods again. I make a plate and offer it to her, but she shakes her head no. She doesn't eat much lately so she's lost some weight and I hate it, but again I don't say anything. Sitting down on the couch at the opposite end, I eat my own food and stare at her. She works for a minute until her phone rings. I watch her face light up as she looks at the screen, and it hurts that it's no longer me putting that beautiful as fuck smile on that perfect face.

"Hey babe!" She answers excitedly. A beat passes before she smiles and says, "Yeah, I'll be right down." Closing her computer, she smiles from ear to ear. Slipping on her shoes and grabbing her purse, she walks toward me. Her hands curl under my arms, pressing herself into my back over the couch as I hear her sigh.

Kissing me softly she says, "I love you baby, even though you don't think I should. I love you even though you feel you hate yourself, and I love you even when you feel like hating me too."

With one last kiss on my neck, she leaves me. My heart squeezes painfully and the need to have another drink settles in my gut. Fuck, I hate myself.

Nothing that happened that night ruined me or us.... His guilt did

that.

2
Changes

Lil

I've had enough change in my life recently to last me a goddamn lifetime. I've lost my mom, I found out my psycho ex-boyfriend didn't really get his brains blown out and decided to come back to life and kidnap me. Oh, and not to mention being beaten, shot, and almost dying, but you know what? I move the fuck on. The big change since is Tank. I want as much normal as I can stand, but he's made that impossible for me. I want everything to go back to before that night, but that's the thing with change, you can't control the turn it takes. You can only move forward and hope for the best as you go.

That night changed me. It was terrible, painful, and so goddamn scary. But in the end, I was alive. I'm thankful for every day I get and I will live every fucking second of it the way I want to. That night could have ended differently, but by some miracle, it didn't. I know it affected everyone 'cause I can see it, feel it, and hear it when they all look at me, but I push through it. We all do what we have to. We all move forward and live, except for Tank.

Since being out of the hospital, I moved in with Tank. I thought we would move on and work toward getting back to our lives together, but instead it's only become a daily struggle. I don't know what else I can possibly do anymore to prove to him that he couldn't have prevented any of it, so I push through because I love him.

I started teaching an online college class and tutoring. It's not exactly what I want to be doing, but it's getting me closer to my end goal. It also gets me out of the house, the club, and gets me around different people. It stifles the need to head back to the city. I'm still working the books, and all the paperwork because it has to be done, at least until I can find someone else I trust to do it for me.

Happy and Mini got a divorce. She left him here heartbroken and lonely. He's not the same man he once was and I hate her for that. I hate that she broke him. He doesn't spend much time with me anymore 'cause he's usually off on runs, on top of a new club whore, or sitting at the bar with Leo. I hope he'll come back soon 'cause I miss him.

Gin *finally* asked Peaches to marry him and I couldn't be happier. They've climbed mountains to get here. After that night, Gin seemed to make a change. We are now in the throes of planning a huge biker wedding with Peaches being the bitchy bridezilla I always knew she would be. She wants flowers and silk, Gin wants leather and beer. I think we all know Peaches will win the wedding battle.

Arms and Melli had a beautiful baby girl named Chloe. No one knew they were expecting, not even them. Tag is still looking for Mrs. Right, and his daughter Dallas is here too. She's a sweet little thing. Stitch and Cali are the same free loving, wild souls. Everyone is still living their lives, doing the best they can.

Two prospects have patched in, Kash and Blade. Blade's fun with his sense of humor and smart-ass mouth. He's a good guy and fits in with this crowd nicely. I'm still not sure how I feel about Kash. He doesn't talk much, but Tank says he's loyal, smart, tough, and all in for his brothers. In Tank's opinion, that's all that matters to the guys.

Since they patched in the two prospects, the guys are recruiting for new ones. I'll never quite understand the allure of being a prospect. It's hard grunt work with little respect, long, excruciating hours, and pretty much zero down time. I've never seen a prospect "enjoy" being a prospect, but the thing I do get is the brotherhood they're working so hard to be a part of. You join the club, you're joining a family. We're as tight as they come and I can see why someone would want to be a part of this, because this is a family I would love and fight with till my last breath.

One of the biggest changes that's happened is that Tank has become acting President of the Hell's Disciples. My dad is still the President and running everything, but he wanted Tank to cover the shit he can't, and for good reason. Shit really unraveled in the club a month after I came home. Things fell apart, while Tank *tried* to pick up the pieces.

Dad and I were the only people inside the club, which wasn't uncommon during the day. He found me at the bar going through the alcohol stock orders. I knew the moment he sat down on the stool next to me that something was wrong. His eyes were haunted and he looked tired and worn out. Not only that, he looked grim and defeated. I'd been having a bad feeling for a while now, but when I saw him, I knew something wasn't right.

He told me he waited until everyone was out 'cause he didn't want any of the guys to hear or see. He told me he was tired of running, tired of hiding. Said he missed mom so much that life just wasn't worth fighting for without her here. Since she died, I was all he had left and he knew I didn't need him like I used to. He said Tank would take care of me, the family, and the club. I couldn't say anything, so I just sat there and listened.

I was watching my hard as nails, tough guy dad give up. He'd said he'd gotten everything in order, that everything was handled, and that I would be okay. He'd left money in the safe at home for me. He put the houses, businesses, bikes and cars in my name. He said I could do with them what I wanted, but he hoped I'd keep them alive and thriving. I watched his eyes water as he tried to hold it in. My heart broke for my dad. I waited for him to just say the words because part of me wanted to hear them, but the other part was terrified. I watched as he got off the stool to hug me, something he rarely did.

"I love you, doll face. Always will. Hold this place down for your old man, yeah?" All I could do was stare at him, a bit in shock. I couldn't speak so in return, I could only nod.

With a hard knock on the door, I watched him open it up to Officer Brad Willis and Sheriff Anderson. That's when it hit me and everything that he said started to sink in. I knew what he was doing.

"Mr. Cruz, please come with us. You're under arrest for the murders of Tom Harris, Mike Sawyer, Ronald Miller, and Joshua Keller."

I watched my dad put his hands behind his back willingly. That fight he always had in him was nowhere to be found. I knew he didn't kill Josh, because I did, and as soon as I opened my mouth to say as much and put a stop to this, he gave me a look that effectively shut me up. Instead I listened as they read him his rights and cuffed him. I was speechless and heartbroken, and I'd just lost him too. Both Officer Willis and Sheriff Anderson gave me a sad nod before ushering my dad through the door in handcuffs.

"I love you too, Daddy."

With one final look, he smiled at me and said, "Hold it down around here for me baby. Keep those boys in check."

Currently Dad is awaiting trial on four counts of murder in the first degree and a handful of other charges. Extortion, money laundering, racketeering, possession of illegal firearms, the illegal distribution and sale of narcotics and firearms, and the list goes on. He's taking it all. He won't give up his brothers so all that shit falls on him. He's facing life, plus two. It's not looking good and it hasn't gotten easier, I've just learned to be numb to it. I never knew how much I needed him until he was gone. I never realized how much I leaned on him for his quiet moral support until he was no longer there. He was always on my side, just as mom was. Now it's me and I need to find a way to be okay with that. I still have the rest of my family and together we'll figure all this shit out. We'll push through 'cause there is no other choice.

Club life has slowly kept moving forward with Tank at the helm and my dad's still running things behind the scenes. I see him trying desperately to keep things normal for everyone. Even though Tank is a natural leader, I notice he doesn't seem to want it. I watch him battle everything in his life right now. It breaks my fucking heart that I can't help him, but he won't let me, he won't even acknowledge it. He's not the same man I met all those months ago. There's something missing in him now, and all I want is for him to come back to me. I need him to move on with me.

Loving Tank right now is a struggle. One minute his love is obsessive and needy, to the point of suffocating. The next, I have to search for it, beg him to give it to me. He doesn't hate me. Deep down in his heart, I know he loves me, but fuck, it's so hard to remember that when he shuts me out. He doesn't talk to me often, he hardly even looks at me. When he fucks me, it's either with desperation or complete vengeance, like he's trying to punish the both of us. If it's not any of these things, he's not around at all.

His constant need to push me away hurts worse than anything that happened to me that night or any other time in my life. It's been months and things haven't gotten better, if anything they've only gotten worse. I'm thankful every fucking day for *my* life, for my time with my loved ones, and mostly for my time with Tank. But for Tank, he can't seem to get past that night. I'm still here, and I plan to fight tooth and nail to bring him back to me. I will not lose him.

I've finally come to the conclusion that he's the only one who can fix himself. There is nothing left that I can do. Instead of bitching, complaining, or whining about it, I just live my life. I stand by him and offer whatever he'll take from me. I also remind myself to have patience. He saw something terrible and that will take time to get over. I go on with my days and act like everything is fine. All I can do is love him and I do that every goddamn minute of every day.

****

"Hey, bitch." Peaches chirps and grins wildly at me as soon as I sit my ass down in her car.

"Why are you cheesin' at me? You're kinda freakin' me out." She looks like she's up to somethin', and if that's the case, then trouble will follow soon after. She just laughs and throws the car in reverse as I stare at her. Pulling out of Tank's driveway, she burns rubber like a nut and throws out a deuce when Tank glares at her from the front door.

"Peaches! What the fuck are you up to?" I implore, throwing an elbow into her side.

She laughs again and says, "Not a damn thing. Just excited to get a new car, girl."

I'm not sure why she needs a new car in the first place. This one is pretty damn new, but that's Peaches for ya.

"So, what kinda car do you want?" Her eyes light up at the question.

"Somethin' pretty n' shiny, fast n' expensive." Peaches says with her high wattage smile. Gin's paying, she's getting something expensive regardless of her need for it. But if you got it like that, hell, I can't blame her.

"I'm down for somethin' fast. I wanna test drive something new too." I tell her. Her ass is not hogging up all the new car fun.

Hell, I should get me a new car. Something pretty and sparkly might put that same smile on me that Peaches is wearing. I need some happy.

"Tank's still bein' a fuckin' moron I take it?" She asks with a cautious sideways glance. Everyone tiptoes around the topic of Tank and I, but not Peaches. She cuts right to it. Just hearing his name hits a painfully raw spot in my heart. Shrugging it off, I stare out the window, hoping my lack of response stops her right here, but that would be too fucking easy, right? She doesn't know how to leave things alone.

"Baby, he'll come 'round. If not, we'll make his ass come back 'round."

I wish it was that easy. I've been trying, but not a damn thing I do seems to make a fuck of a difference to him.

"Not so sure about that, but I can keep hoping." Is my only response.

Giving me a wicked smile, Peaches adds, "We'll bring his ass back 'round, one way or another baby girl."

3
Hospitals

Tank

Sitting at the bar at the club, I hold my old friend Jack. He and I go way back. I'm sitting there takin' shots when Rampage and Gin come grumbling into the room, bitching about somethin' or other. I just don't give a fuck enough to ask.

"Sick of your shit," Gin says sitting down next to me. I guess I won't have to ask.

"Yeah? Why the fuck should I care what you're sick of?" Instantly I regret my words. Goddamn it. It isn't his fault I'm losing my mind and my shit. On top of my fucked up shit with Lil, I've got club shit to deal with too. I feel like I'm drowning in the middle of the ocean with no life vest and the coast guard is days out. I don't want it all, but I'm too much of an asshole to let it all go. I used to want this shit, but now? I can barely stomach it.

"Get that you've had some fucked up shit happen, but fuck. You're not the only one asshole. It happened to me too. You don't see the rest of us bein' a bunch of bitches 'bout it. Been month's man, now it's time to move the fuck on. Tired of cleanin' up your messes."

"Wasn't your girl's blood you had to wash off your hands. Wasn't your girl you had to watch die. Don't wanna hear shit about how it affected you." I'm so fucking tired of everyone not seeing this shit.

"She ain't fuckin' dead, you dumbass motherfucker, but you sure as fuck act like she is." Gin shoves away from the bar and gives me a nasty glare. I know he's sick of it. How the fuck does he think I feel?

"Don't think I won't put your ass on the ground. Remember, you're the *acting President*, which won't hold shit when Low finds out you're fucking up club shit. Might want to check your shit before you come up in here actin' like a bitch."

Rampage shakes his head at me with nothin' but disgust. So sick and fuckin' tired of the looks, the whispers, and the drama.

"What?" I snap at Rampage, who's also giving me the stare down.

"Damn, brother. You need to pull it together or you're gonna lose everything. We're all just sitting back watching your shit slip right through your fuckin' fingers. It' all on you."

Fuck him. Fuck this whole goddamn place. Snatching up a bottle, I hit the office and sit down to drink all this shit into oblivion ... alone. Then, I get the phone call .... Knew it was coming.

****

This place bothers the fuck out of me. Not gonna lie, it makes me nervous as fuck. A loud metal sound clicks when the heavy door is released to swing open. Then it's the same loud click locking you inside the impenetrable walls of hell. Walking through the doors, you always have that brief, but ever present sense of dread and regret. You think "Holy fuckin' shit! I just walked through these doors and they may never let me out." I never should have come, but here I am anyway.

We had to pull some serious strings to get me in here. Low insisted I come, and if he wouldn't have pushed, I wouldn't be here. It's business as usual when I reach check in. I.D., metal detector, pat down, I.D. check again, the rule spiel, another metal detector, I.D. check, and then I'm finally seated at a small cubical thing with its bulletproof glass between us and a hard plastic stool under my ass. As we were granted this visit, I still have my own personal bodyguard standing behind me. With his arms crossed over his chest, he thinks he looks like a bad ass. His badge is shined up all nice, catching the florescent lights. Fucking idiot. I could kill him with his own government issued gun if I was lookin' for a fight.

Low shuffles his shackled feet toward me. His arms are securely cuffed behind his back. He looks rough and tired, in need of a shave and a good night's sleep. With a serious head nod, he sits down and picks up the phone, as I pick up mine. I get no *hey's* or *how are you's.* This is serious business.

"Been hearin' rumors deep in here brother." Prisons are like fucking high school. News travels quickly from the outside to the inside. And inside, news makes the rounds even quicker.

"Yeah?" He needs to just get to the point.

"Yeah. Don't like hearin' them rumors in here when I left you out there to handle business." He's gonna drag this out? I don't have the time or patience for riddles and talking in circles.

"You got issues, say 'em. Didn't come for games, Low." He tilts his head to the side and gives the guard behind me a quick jerk of his head. The guy takes a few steps back and turns around. Even in here this motherfucker has pull.

"First off, lock down that line with Rick. He knows it's gonna be a seventy/thirty split. Money before product. Don't let him jump the gun with that shit either." He may be in prison, but he's still running the show. Fine, whatever. I'll get shit handled.

"Now to the bigger issue." Here it goes.

"Let you have her, brother. Even gave you my blessin'. You spittin' on that blessin'?"

Not sure what he wants me to say to that shit. Does he want me to tell him that I love his daughter so goddamn much I would die without her? Does he want to know that when I look at her it makes me sick to my stomach? Does he want to hear me say I fuck her so hard sometimes I fucking hurt her in the process of trying to punish myself? Not that I would tell him that shit, but he's not gonna let me say anything anyway.

"Heard you been shruggin' your responsibilities off."

What? Did Lil tattle to Daddy? Just as that thought crosses my mind, he gives me a look. He knows exactly what the fuck I'd just thought. He's like a fucking mind reader.

"Get that thought out of your motherfuckin' head. Ya know she doesn't say shit, but she's my fuckin' baby and I can hear it when she talks, no matter how fucking fine she tries to sound. I know it's you. Gin, Stitch, n' Rampage let me know. Yeah they rat 'cause they love her and she's fuckin' miserable. They've also been taking up all the slack at the club 'cause you're ass is always so goddamn drunk. You're letting your brothers down, and I will not hesitate to order a whip ass for ya to get you back in fuckin' line. You got issues with that, take it up with them."

Fucking assholes. What's that stupid saying? Bro's before ho's? I don't need the daddy lectures or told how to run the fuckin' club. I know what the fuck is going on.

"Listen, I'll handle mine, don't worry about it." I answer.

He just shakes his head. "Don't sound like you're handlin' shit."

"You worry about gettin' your charges dropped."

Jumping out of his seat, the chair goes flying backwards and he gives me the stare down. His anger is flaring in his eyes, but there isn't a goddamn thing he can do about it behind that glass. "Handle *your* motherfuckin' responsibilities. Take care of your brother's n' your woman. You take care of *my* goddamn daughter and *my* goddamn club, or I will take care of you. Feel me?"

****

"Wake your ass up!" The chair jerks away from the desk, making my head fall off my hands and land on the desk with a thud. Dammit. After that fun little visit with Low, I came in here and threw myself a little party.

"The fuck?" I grumble at the soon to be hurting asshole.

"Get the fuck up. Girls were in an accident."

The word accident echoes around in the sudden silence as my heart stops. Rampage is standing over me looking pissed off and irritated. Pushing off the desk and chair, I get up, but not before knocking the bottle of Canadian Whiskey off the desk. The second I stand up, I start to sway on my feet. I lean on the desk to keep my ass upright.

"What a stupid, goddam fuckin' asshole," Rampage

mutters before stomping through the door without a second look.

Stumbling into the main room, Gin is already at the door

and ready to go. That hopeless panic and alcohol coursing through

me makes it hard to function. I can barely see straight, let alone

think straight.

"What the fuck happened?"

Tossing my phone at me, Gin growls, "If ya woulda

answered your fuckin' phone, you would know Peaches was t-

boned while she was test drivin'." His words leave a sickening hole

in my gut.

"Fuck. Lil? Is she okay?" Shrugging his shoulders, he

pushes through the door, leaving me alone to process his words

through the fog of alcohol.

The whole ride to the hospital I feel sick and crazy. I fight

not to pull over and throw the fuck up. My mind is still hazy as shit

from the Whiskey and I sure as fuck shouldn't be driving like this, but Gin left my ass to worry about it. So here I am again, letting Lil down. I'm so fuckin' selfish that I had a pity party for myself and passed out. I was so out of it that I didn't hear the phone ring when she called and needed me.

The need to get to her has me running red lights, blowing stop signs, and cuttin' people off. Pulling up to the hospital, I park in the loading zone, start heading in while I struggle to keep my shit in check. My heart is beating out of my chest while my hands shake uncontrollably. Walking in through the sliding glass doors, I give the honking and screaming bitch in the minivan the finger. Stupid ass bitch.

"I need to see my girl." I tell some old bitch at the front desk. The waiting room is filled with hushed murmurs as people in the waiting room instantly look away from the drunk biker. They cautiously watch me from under their hats, through their lashes, or sideways glances. This shit is nothin' new. It makes me fucking crazy, but I don't got time for that shit now.

"What is her name please?"

The women at the registration desk just stares at her computer, completely oblivious to my near meltdown right here in front of her desk. I'm close to strangling this bitch if she doesn't hurry.

"Lil."

A few clicks on the computer and she tells me, "There's no one here with that name sir."

"The fuck there isn't. Check again." Raising her black, thickly rimmed eyes to me, she gives me a nasty once over while her fingers are tapping impatiently on her desk. This bitch doesn't know she is one fuckin' second away from me beating her motherfucking ass, woman be damned.

"Sir, I told you there is no one here with that name."

"Look for Lilly Cruz," Gin says calmly from beside me. Fuck. I can't handle this shit.

Being in the hospital makes me queasy and jumpy. I hate the smell and the way everyone here looks somber and sad. This shit brings me right back to waiting for Lil to die on me that night. It brings me right back to desperately praying by her side, begging and pleading to have my baby be okay. Everything about this place sends me right back, and reminds me of my failure. I fucking hate this place.

4
Captain Dick Face

Lil

I'm sitting here on the side of the hospital bed as I watch my feet dangle above the floor. I really hate these hospital gowns. They could, at the very least, have a back on them. Why an open back? I mean, I could see the point if you had an issue with your back, but what if you've got an issue with your front? What then? Stupid ass hospital gowns. I'm guessing a man designed them.

"Imma slip mine around so the back is in the front. Ya know, give the hot doctor a little show." Peaches says from the bed across from me while wiggling her eyebrows.

"Or a heart attack. He looks like he's gay," I counter. Throwing her head back, she laughs.

"Either way," she says giving me a lazy shrug. "You'd really give him a show if ya just got totally naked."

"Yeah, but he'd probably call in security and my ass would get arrested and exiled from the hospital." That's all I would need. Arrested for purposely flashing a doctor.

A loud commotion comes from the hall, people shouting and yelling.

"Here comes crazy." Peaches announces. Instantly I know who it is. No need to see, only Tank would bring that much commotion with him. When Peaches called Gin, she explained everything to him so I know he's not freaking out. That can only leave one person.

The door kicks open and Tanks panic-stricken self comes stomping into the room in a fury. His fists are flying and his feet are stomping. I can only see his cut covered back, but I know he's close to killing every person in here. I know he's drunk, which has him barely hanging on.

"Don't give 'a fuck if I'm not married to her or related, she's my Old Lady. Education for your ass. You try n' remove me from this motherfuckin' hospital, I will snap your neck n' burn this place down!" He shouts in a man's face. Some big guy in a lab coat tries to grab him, and of course, Tank just shoves him out of his way like the guy weighs nothing.

"Tank! Please calm down. Look at me, I'm fine." Those wild blue eyes find me, and something along the lines of terror and anger stare back at me. Tearing back the hospital curtain, he barges his way into the room to get to me.

"Jesus fuckin' Christ! What the fuck happened?"

"Some old fart in a station wagon t-boned that cute little Benz I was drivin'," Peaches pouts at Gin. God she will not stop talking about that damn car. "I liked that one too, boo boo." she whimpers pathetically.

He just ignores her comment and hands her her shoes, looking completely annoyed and tired.

"Put your shit on babe so we can get the hell out of here. Not in the mood to go to jail today."

"But I liked that car baby," she whines at him again. She's really putting on a show. She told the doctor she needed pain meds. She even told the nurse she's going to need a wheelchair to get to the truck. Lazy, spoiled bitch.

Gin waved off the wheelchair. "Gotcha n' I'll get ya one just like it if ya shut the fuck up 'bout it."

Giving my forehead a kiss, Gin grumbles down at me.

"You gonna be okay with Captain Dick Face over there?" he nods over at Tank who's having a mental break down in the corner. He keeps going back and forth between sitting and standing, pulling on his hair and looking like a fucking lunatic who didn't take his meds.

Nodding at Gin, I can only roll my eyes. "Yeah I'm good. I'll see ya in the morning."

Gin scoops Peaches up bride style and heads for the door while she throws a wicked grin over his shoulder at me, she says to him in her sweet baby voice, "Baby, my back hurts. You gonna rub it for me at home?" That little shithead.

"Night babe," I tell her before they leave.

"Night sweet cheeks," she calls back before they're through the door.

****

"Can't handle this fuckin' shit. Always worryin'. Always drivin' myself crazy." Tank rants as he paces back and forth in the living room. Jesus, we just walked in the front door. I barely made it to the couch before he was having a fucking break down.

"I'm gonna end up dead."

Yes, he is. I'm going to kill him my damn self.

He can't take it? What the fuck did I do? I tip toe around him, cater to him every second of the day. I always keep my mouth shut and smile when I really want to kick him in his fucking ass. I try everything to make this all easier on *him*.

"You can't take what? My love, my loyalty? Please be more specific." I know I'm picking a fight, but Christ, doesn't he see that this shit is hard on me too? It's not always only about him.

"Every fuckin' thing," he yells as he pulls at his hair. "Every goddamn thing Lilly. I just can't take worryin' somethin' is gonna happen to you. I can't live like this."

So, he can't live like this? Join my club. I've been living *with* this. I've been living with his special brand of crazy for so fucking long, putting up with his needy ass. I've done it all with a smile and shoulder to lean on. I put *my* shit aside to help him though all of this. Sometimes I just want to scream "WHAT ABOUT ME?" Sometimes I just want to pack my shit and run. I shouldn't have to hold his hand through every single thing, but I do. I do it because I fucking love him.

"You're worried about the wreck?" He looks at me like the question is completely stupid, like my words make no damn sense.

He's really making a bigger deal than necessary over this accident though. If he weren't so fucking drunk, he would know that we were going fifteen miles an hour through the intersection. The old guy was turning at the wrong time and hit us, at like five miles an hour. The car doesn't even have a dent, only a long scratch. The dealership insisted we be checked out for insurance purposes only. Life happens. I don't know what he wants me to do. Never leave the house? Fuck, maybe I should take up residency in a goddamn bubble attached to him.

It's not just what happened today though. I know it's not. It's so much fucking bigger. It's so big it's beyond me now. The accident isn't what's caused this, it's what is bringing all the shit to the surface. This has been building, and he's letting this shit weigh on him and it's taking its toll. It's wearing him down. Fuck, it's wearing me down.

"Tank I'm fine. You're gettin' upset for no reason."

"For no reason?" He says quietly; too damn quietly. I'm not sure what's scarier. Tank being loud and raging or when he's quite and subdued.

"Yes Tank, no reason. You've been drinking and maybe that has you like this, but everything is fine, okay?"

"Fuck Lil! You just don't fuckin' get it." He explodes.

My heart twists in my chest. I know he's going through something, but he won't let me in. He won't let me try to help so I have no clue where to go from here. I can only stay at home so much before it wears on me, and I can only reassure him so much until it becomes just background noise. Nothing I do or say works, so I don't say anything. I just stare at him and watch him slowly kill himself with worry.

"Then help me. Help me get it Tank!" He only shakes his head. His face falls before he opens the door and walks through it without a second look. He shuts me out. Again.

****

The room tips slightly. The floor feels sloped and uneven under my extremely heavy feet, but my body sways unprovoked to the music. God I hate this fucking song, but I can't stop myself. If I close one eye, and squint the other one, the man I'm dancing with kind of looks like the thirty year old cowboy version of George Clooney. This was a good idea six shots of Jose ago. Tank left, so I called Peaches and she brought me here. Now my dancing partner's too-tight Levis covered dick is pressing into my thigh and his small hands are roaming places that are going to get them removed.

Why I said yes to Peaches, I'll never know. She said shots and I was game. Probably not the best idea 'cause drinking while on emotional overload never ends well.

"Thanks for the dance." I try to smile at him, but I'm sure it's looking more like a squeamish, half-assed lip curl.

I dodge grabby hands and head for the bar. I plant my ass on the stool next to Peaches and she looks at me for a second before we both burst into a crazy drunk cackle, hanging onto the bar and hanging off one another.

"Haha! How'd ya like his jeans?" She laughs while thrusting at me like a fucking pervert. I can only roll my eyes, well at least try to roll them anyway.

"I think they were tighter than your jeans." I'm surprised she can move in those things.

"But they were so fuckin' sexy," she deadpans. I can't hold it. I laugh until my sides hurt and I have tears rolling down my cheeks. This is why I said yes … I needed this. I needed it so fucking desperately. We both just keep laughing until Peaches face sobers and her eyes narrow.

"Jesus Christ, I told them it was girls night."

Turning my head, I see Tank walking toward me. He reaches me in a few swaggered steps and his body is instantly on mine. Leaning into my side, he sets his rough hand obscenely high on my thigh. His fingers are pretty fucking close to my panties and digging into my skin, which makes my skin tingle and my blood heat. I know that look in his eyes. This is when he wants me. This is a small piece of the old Tank I miss so fucking much. I'll take this Tank even if it is alcohol induced and only lasts for a short time. I'll take him however I can get him anymore.

"Need you baby," he whispers roughly in my ear, biting down on my ear lobe, hard.

I give him a smile and tell him, "Let's go."

****

"Lean over that table, baby," Tanks gruff deep voice says against my neck, right below my ear. That sexy as fuck scruff on his face is rubbing roughly on my neck, causing some pain. His chest and stomach are pressed into my naked back while my hips are pushed into the table and my ass is in the air. The soft material of his shirt rubbing on my back gives me goose bumps. I shiver involuntarily as he kisses the scar on my back, running his tongue over my skin.

"Never understand why the fuck you love me baby." He growls softly, sounding pained. I wish he wouldn't say things like that. It breaks my heart.

Running his hand through my hair, he wraps it around his hand and roughly pulls my head back onto his shoulder. His other hand is at the base of my neck, his thumb running back and forth lightly. "But you do n' I thank fuck every day for that shit."

"Fuck Tank. *Please.*" He moves his hand that's not holding my hair to my hip, gripping it so tight I feel his fingernails bite into my skin. He pounds harder into me as my legs shake and my body tightens. Kicking my feet further apart, he thrusts even deeper. He starts gliding his hand from my hip, up my stomach to my tits, grabbing a handful and painfully, he squeezes hard. The table legs scrape on the floor while I fight not to want this, but my body fights harder and it wins; it wants this and it gives into him. He's so rough, and pounding into me so hard, I know he'll leave bruises. He buries himself deep inside me with each fierce hit.

"Give ... it ... up ... for ... me." Pushing into me, I hear a sharp hiss leave his clenched jaw. Shit starts to go fuzzy on me. My eyes fight to roll back into my head and my legs want to give out on me.

"Damn. *Please.* Fuck. ... Fuck baby," Pulling on my hips, he reaches down to lift one leg higher, getting a better angle to go even deeper. I'm so fucking wet that it's running down my thigh. His hard, rough hand lands on my ass with a sting. Biting down on my lip, Tank bites my shoulder and I lose it. I let it all go. "Fuckin' Christ baby." Slamming into me, he's relentless. "Tell me this pussy is mine, Lil." he demands with another hard slap. "Say it baby!"

"Fuck. It's yours, it's always fucking yours ... *fuck.*"

"That's right baby. All fucking mine till the day I die."

****

Lying in bed I can't sleep. I know it's got to be at least two in the morning, and Tank's been gone for hours now. He fucked me, then he left. This is nothing new. It used to make me feel used and cheap, but after a few months of it, I've just grown numb to it like everything else in my life right now. I tried to call his phone, but of course, he turned it off. I called the club looking for him and Leo said he was around there somewhere. I didn't want to talk to him, I just wanted to make sure he was okay. I hate this wedge he insists on driving between us. He's always holding every unforeseen accident and lurking danger against me. He knows that he's tearing us apart, but he doesn't seem to care.

I'm scared shitless when I hear my phone ring from the nightstand, waking me from a restless sleep a while later.

"Hello?"

"Aye sis. Get down here n' get him before I kill him." Gin growls into the phone, clearly pissed off.

"Okay," I sigh. I just don't have the fight in me anymore. Before all this, I would have told Gin to deal with it, but no one but me wants to deal with him anymore. I'm getting too tired of this shit myself.

"Sis?" He calls before I can hang up.

"Yeah?"

"None of this is your fault, ya know that, right? It's his issue, his problem. This is all Tanks fuck up."

Is it though? I want to believe him. I want his words to be the truth, but they're not. He wouldn't be feeling this way if it weren't for me. I know it's not my fault, but I do know I inadvertently played a hand in it.

"Okay."

****

I finally got him into the house. It took Stitch and Rampage thirty minutes to convince him to get in the car with me when I showed up. He kept saying things like, "Why would I go with that bitch? She ruined my life." Or, "I can't even look at her. I love her so much it makes me sick." How could that shit not hurt. The way he looked at me with such disdain killed me. They always say you speak the truth when you're drunk.

In my heart, I know he's speaking from the heart. I know he feels that way; he doesn't even have to say it 'cause I can see it in his eyes when he does look at me. I also know he loves me, but struggles with it. This is a losing battle for the both of us now. I finally see it.

"C'mere baby," he grumbles at me from the doorway while I slip my clothes back off.

"You should try and get some sleep." I tell him when he sways on his feet and holds onto the doorframe. He's leaning against the door shirtless, his jeans unbuttoned, and his boots missing as he stares holes though me with that look in his eyes. He's not too drunk to get undressed, but he's too drunk to reason with.

"Not fuckin' sleep babe. I wanna fuck my woman again."

I should have left him at the club. I should have let Gin just beat him.

"Tank you're drunk," I tell him like he doesn't already know. I'm stalling. I'm trying to push back the inevitable where I let him love me his way and then leave me feeling like shit.

"Yeah, n' you should shut the fuck up n' finish gettin' naked."

I never thought I'd be here with him. I never thought I'd love someone so much, yet hate them at the same time. He's driving me to resent him. He's pushing that hate into my heart. I've always wanted him. Since the moment we met, I've wanted him in my life. I always want him fucking me, I would have never turned him down. Now it just scares me. Will this last time be it?

Will this last time be the time my love crumbles completely? Will this be the time he ruins me forever.

I don't know how we got here. How did I let him drift so far away from me? I go to him again anyway. No matter how much we hate each other on the surface, deep down there's love. Deep down there's so much more.

Walking toward him, I know I can't do it anymore. In my heart I can't do this every day for the rest of my life. I can't do it to myself or to him anymore. It's not fair to either of us, but for tonight I can't tell him no, no matter how much it hurts to say yes.

5
Dirty Sheets

Tank

I wake up alone in bed. I fucking hate that shit. Not waking up to her body near mine instantly sends my mood to shit. Sitting up, I look over to her side of the bed. The sheet is tore away from the mattress, and clothes are thrown all over the place. The comforter is barely hanging on to the edge of the bed 'cause most of it's on the floor. A little bit of her makeup is smeared on her pillow.

I watched her dance in that bar last night. That body of hers so goddamn hypnotizing and sinful I had to fuck her. Then I fucked her again after she brought me back home. I watched that little shit play grab ass with my girl. I didn't like it, but she pushed him away with a face smothered in pure disgust, so I let it be. I let it be, because I was hungry for her. I needed her and I knew if I killed that little cowboy puke, Lil would have made me work for it.

I wasn't in the mood to work for it, so I was good, got her home

and fucked her. I fucked her, and because I felt guilty, I had a

drink. Then I felt guilty for leaving her in bed so I fucked her again.

Thinking about Lil last night, my cock starts to throb

painfully. She was so goddamn perfect bent over that table for

me, letting me fuck her the only way I can anymore. Taking

everything from her like I always do. I can see that long dark hair

laying down her back, soft and smooth, begging to be wrapped

around my hand, her legs shaking and her body shivering against

mine as I sink into her over and over again. Her pussy is tight and

warm, gripping the fuck out of my dick as I pound into her balls

deep. She screams, moans and begs for me. No matter how many

times, how many ways, or where I fuck her, it's like the first time.

So fucking good it makes my balls ache and my toes curl just

thinking about it. It makes me want to find her, throw her down,

and sink my dick into her again.

Walking into the kitchen, I hear female voices followed by Lil's laugh. That's the easy going, soft laugh that I never get from her anymore.

"How you doin' darlin'?" That'd be Kiki. I hear Lil sigh, and that sigh says more than words. That's a sad, tired sigh. I shouldn't listen because I don't wanna hear a damn thing these bitches have to say about me or my fuckin' relationship. They'll say shit they don't know a goddamn thing about.

"I'm alright." Lil tries to sound fine, but it's there in her voice.

"You don't sound alright, baby. He still not being the man he needs to be for ya?" I wait for the shit Lil's about to spill about me. I know she wants to.

"We'll be okay." Nothing. Shit is falling down around her and she still pretends that shit's okay. Even though everyone, including me, can see it and feel it, she won't say a word against me. She lets that shit sit and eat away at her, but I let her deal with it all.

"You ain't gottao pretend with me baby. I know, hell, we all know he's lost his ever lovin' mind." Fucking Kiki talking about shit she knows nothing about. She's recently started giving me hell, puttin' her nose in our business. She's dumb as shit if she thinks her opinion matters.

"Things are strained. He's had a lot to deal with, but it'll get better," Lil says softly.

"Strained?" Kiki repeats. I can hear her disbelief. I know they care about Lil, but these bitches thrive off drama.

"Yes, strained. It fuckin' sucks, but we'll work through it." The lack of conviction in Lil's words hurt. I know she's just spitting shit to satisfy these nosy bitches. She says whatever she thinks they need to hear from her, and I know she doesn't believe a goddamn word of it herself.

"Personally I'd scrape him off," Mary adds in. Fucking bitches trying to turn my Old Lady away from me. Fuck these stupid bitches.

"I can't."

"Why not? He's not treatin' you the way he should, then let him go. Haven't you had enough of his shit? You're the one who's been through all the shit, not him. He needs to let go and get the fuck over it. Your ass is here, alive. He needs to take advantage of that instead of blaming you for him feeling like a fuck up." I've never wanted to strangle Mary as much as I do right now.

"Don't you get it? I love him, that's why."

"Oh, I don't know Lil. I used to see how he looked at you. He loves you, but he's just so lost." There's Melli. I got the whole goddamn flock in my kitchen telling my woman what they want her to do.

"Fuck that, he ain't treatin' you right honey. Stop pretendin' it's gonna be okay. Don't let him run you down 'cause I know damn well Lucy would hate to see this."

"Mary's got a point. Don't let him wear you down baby. No one is worth it if you just end up losin' yourself in the process. You may never come back from it."

Lil's voice is nowhere to be heard in this whole conversation now. I listen to them all give their opinion. Some good, most just fucking bullshit. Either way, it ain't shit I wanna hear.

****

Where the fuck is she? I can't fucking find her!

I left her in the kitchen with those bitches and now no one knows where the fuck she is. Her cell goes straight to voicemail and the Jeep is in my motherfucking driveway. The front door's unlocked but there's no Lil. She sure the fuck ain't at home. I

checked that motherfucker. Searched the entire fucking place by

tearing it apart.

She's not at the club. I searched every room, grilled

everyone. She's not at the school. Those stupid bitches said they

left Lil at home in her pj's, now no one seems to know a goddamn

thing. I feel fucking crazy. I feel like the night Josh took her from

me and I feel so fucking helpless. Fuck! She's gone.

"What'd she say she was doin'?" I ask Melli for the third

time. I moved onto her after Peaches called me a fucking prick

and took a swing at me. Cali threw a pool ball at me, and Kiki

slammed the swinging kitchen door in my face. Wasn't in the

mood to start killing bitches right this second, but that shit could

change because I doubt those fucking bitches would tell me even

if they knew.

Melli's sitting on a stool and I'm standing over her, trying

to scare the fuck out of her. She's scared, but it's not scared enough to get her talking. Bitch looks like she might cry or puke. Her wide eyes look up at me while her hands shake in her lap.

"I … I don't know. She didn't say anything about goin' anywhere. She … uh … She didn't say anything."

"You fuckin' sure? You lyin' to me?" I lean in close to her.

Arms shoots me a look when I yell at his wife. I don't care. Don't give a fuck about anyone but Lil. He wants to get pissy about it, that's fine, I'll handle him after I find Lil's ass.

"Back off, asshole," he warns me.

I walk away and pace, still checking every square inch of the clubs floors. I call her cell every few seconds. I've got Kash at the house waiting and motherfuckers looking around town. The longer I don't know where she is, the sicker I feel. I feel out of control and I hate not knowing where she is. I hate this shit. I hate caring about someone else. Fuck. Fuck. Fuck.

6
Broken Chairs

Lil

"Bye, babe!" I wave back over my shoulder from the front porch. I even send her ass an air kiss like some classy broad.

Lailah laughs and shakes her head at me. "Text you later, cuddle muffin!"

I heave my shopping bags, and myself in through the door. Kicking off my shoes and setting down my bags, I look up when I push the front door closed. My heart stutters in my chest 'cause I find a disaster inside. What the hell happened in here? Were we robbed? Is someone looking for something?

A chill of panic washes over me as I try to push the creeping memories back and hold them down. Josh is dead. Tick is dead. I take some deep breaths and tell myself that a few more times and work hard to shake it off.

A chair is smashed on the ground with pieces of splintered wood all over the floor. Well there goes my new dining room table. The pictures that were once on the wall are now broken and thrown all over the floor, glass cracked and smashed into pieces. The coffee table's on it's top with magazines, books, and mail all over the place, ripped and torn.

Turning back around, the front door is cracked down the middle and there are three fist sized holes punched into the plaster of the wall, streaked with blood. What the fuck happened?

Walking down the hall to the bedroom, it looks just like the living room. Blankets, clothes, and shoes are all over the place, curtains hanging off the rods. I take one more look around and walk back into the front room, feeling stunned and on autopilot. I haven't got the slightest clue what's happened.

Nothing seems to be missing. The TV's, computers, electronics, and expensive shit are still here.

Walking back into the front room, Tank is standing by the door and his face is terrifying. My blood runs cold and my step falters. I instantly take a step back on sheer sight.

His chest is rising and falling with quick, deep breaths. There is something very feral and terrifying in his eyes when he stares back at me, all bloodshot and unfocused. For the first time since I've met Tank, a beat of fear stutters in my heart. His hands are clinching and un-clinching at his sides. There's a slight tremor in his body as he stares at me. I try to smooth my face into something neutral and uncaring, but right now I'm nervous; Nervous he'll be mad, sad, or that he'll just completely go crazy and leave me, maybe worse. Right now he's unpredictable, so I never know what to expect. For the first time, I'm scared of him.

"Tank ...." I speak first. Holding up a hand, he stops me.

"Don't fuckin' say shit to me." Blinking a couple of times, I look around and back at him. Did I miss something?

"Did you do this?" I ignore him and ask anyway. I wave a hand around the mess, like I'm trying to formulate an answer. He dips his head slightly and narrows his glazed eyes at me. I've got no clue what's going on, so I stand still and wait.

"You really disappear on me?" he returns sharply.

"Excuse me?

Disappear? I had lunch with Lailah and we stopped by a few stores. I've been gone for four hours. I hardly call that disappearing on him.

"Disappear," he repeats and does hand gestures like a fucking magician. Is he trying to be funny?

"I'm so completely fuckin' lost Tank. Is this a joke or what? What happened to the house?"

"Jesus fuckin' Christ. JESUS FUCKIN' CHRIST!" He roars and puts another fist through the wall as he walks out the door. I flinch at the loud crack from the wood giving way to flesh, then I watch him walk away, feeling stuck as he once again shuts down and shuts me out.

****

I gave him a few hours. I spent the time cleaning the house, righting furniture and hanging up clothes. For the holes, I wouldn't even know where to start so I leave them for another time. Hang a picture over them? Maybe Gin or Happy could fix them. Hell, I need Bob the fucking builder for that shit. I'll leave them be.

While I picked up and cleaned, I tried to piece together what the fuck all that shit was, but I'm fucking clueless. Part of me thinks it's probably something I wouldn't understand, even if I knew. But my heart wants to know Tank is okay. My heart fights to be there for him no matter what kind of shit he's going through.

Driving down the road toward the club, I think and drive, which is almost as bad as driving and crying. I'm replaying Tanks heartbreaking face when the wheel jerks hard to the right in my hands. My purse topples over and onto the passenger side floorboard, while my cell slides off the seat. Instantly there's a terrible tremor and wobble in my Jeep. Oh good fucking God. You've got to be shitting me? What is it with vehicles and me?

Hanging onto the steering wheel, I pull off toward the shoulder of the road as my jeep comes to a bumpy and unsteady stop. I jump out of the car to see that my poor tire is blown to shreds and the rim is all bent up. Just my fucking luck.

I tug. I wiggle. I kick my tire, but that rim is bent to shit and it's not going anywhere. Why me? Like seriously. I need a fucking drink because this shit is just too much. Sticking my head back inside, I grab my phone and try Tank. Of course his phone is off. I try Gin and get him, thankfully.

"Sis?" Gin answers on the first ring.

"Jeep blew a tire." I tell him. His response is exactly what I expected it would be.   "Change it then." He says lamely, like I didn't think of that already.

"Tried, asshole. The rim is bent. Come get me."

"Alright. 'Bout twenty out."

Leaning against the door, I hear tires crunching on the gravel of the shoulder. Looking behind me, I see a man in a big truck I don't recognize pull up.

"Hey you need a hand?" The guy calls over to me while stepping out of his old beat up Chevy.

Probably not a good idea, but I yell back.

"Uh, yeah. Sure."

Reaching back inside, I grab the small hunting knife from under the seat and tuck it into my pocket. God knows who this guy is and with my luck with men, he's probably a psycho looking for his next kill.

Walking up he says, "Names Mike."

"Lilly." I offer him.

"Had a blowout, I see. The wife had one a few months back and she couldn't get the thing off herself. It was bitch. Need a hand?"

I wave a hand towards the tire, giving him free rein. Why not let him go at it. I got nowhere with it.

"If you want to, but I've got a ride comin'." I tell him.

Partially because it's true and partially because if he wants to kill me, chop me into small pieces and stuff me into a suitcase for later, he might think twice if he knows people will be coming for me.

"Don't mind. Someone helped my wife until I got there. Good road karma." He seems genuine and sincere so I let him help me. Better him getting greasy hands then me anyway.

I left my road side knight and shining armor to do his thing. I was no help so I figure I might as well clean up the contents of my purse that's all over the floor. Seems kind of befitting for the kind of day I'm having. Shit being broken and spilled, and me having to clean them up. Poetic justice, I suppose.

I'm shoving my lip gloss back into my purse when I hear the familiar rumble of pipes. I'm sweeping the rest of my shit back into its home when I hear him. Shit. Shit. Shit.

"Where the fuck's my woman?" Tanks furious voice growls at the man, and he's not sounding happy. Where the fuck did he come from? He wasn't answering his phone. Jesus Christ, his timing is fabulous.

"Uh. *Um*. Yeah she..." Sticking my head around the side of the Jeep, I spot Tank looming over my little helper. God he looks huge next to the small, scared man. My nervous friend Mike glances around. I'm sure he has no clue what's going on and Tank's just staring at him like he might perform magic for him or something.

"Where the fuck is she before I snap your fuckin' neck." Tank threatens the poor guy. Mike steps back and looks around for something to probably bonk Tank over the head with, not that that would stop Tank. He's a man on a mission.

"Calm down Tank. I got a flat and he was nice enough to stop and help me till Gin got here. His name is Mike." Tilting his head around the guy, he gives me a thorough once over. He sees that I'm fine, so now he looks bored and mildly annoyed.

"Mike?" he repeats stupidly. All I do is nod. It doesn't matter what I say, he's gonna be annoyed I'm being helped by a man no matter what his name is. He looks back at Mike, but Mike's staring at me. He looks scared.

"Don't fuckin' look at my Old Lady." Tank snaps at him. Mike glances back at Tank and then back to me. He's clearly not sure what to do or say. Poor guy.

There is no malice or ill will when Mike looks at me. He's completely unsure of what to think or do about Tank. I don't blame him. Tanks scary and I get it, but then I notice Tank. He has that look in his eyes that I've become all too familiar with, and it doesn't look well for Mike. No matter how mad Tank is at me, he won't hesitate to bury someone looking at me in the wrong way. That rigid set to his body as he towers over Mike spells disaster. Mike's going to end up bleeding. Fuck.

I go to grab onto Mike's arm to get him away from killer, but it's too late. Tank punches him square in the face with no hesitation. I hear cartilage crack and skin split as Mike stumbles back helplessly with an agonized groan. Blindly, he stumbles into me and I slip back on the loose gravel and lose my footing. His staggering keeps him falling into me as he tries to steady himself, but it's not working. With nothing to grab onto in front of me, I twist to grab onto the side on the Jeep, but I'm not quick enough.

My temple, down my face to my upper lip meet the side of the

bumper of my Jeep.

"Fuck! Jesus Christ, Lilly." Tank's crouching down in front

of me in an instant. His eyes look wild, but mostly they're lost.

Why? Why does it have to be this way? Why does he have

to act first and ask questions later? He knows damn well Mike is

no threat. I can't handle all the ups and downs anymore. He wants

me and then he has me. He pushes me away, but still wants me.

He doesn't want me, but he won't just let me fucking go.

I'm done walking on egg shells all the time. No one can

look at me. No one can talk to me. He's even getting pushy with

my family. I can't have anyone besides him, yet he doesn't want

anything to do with me. I'm always alone. Does anything that I've

gone through matter at all to him? Losing my mom, my dad in

prison because of me, almost dying, and now living with someone

I have to take care of. I have no one to take care of me or help me through this.

Lifting a hand to my lip, I feel the sticky stain of blood. My lip has a dull throb and it fucking stings.

"Damn baby. Fuck, I'm sorry." Pulling me up to him he buries his face in my neck. "Shit, I lost my shit. You disappeared on me earlier n' now this." I start pushing him off me. Whatever his issues, it's not a good enough excuse for acting like a complete asshole.

"I didn't disappear. I had lunch with Lailah and we went shopping, asshole. I need to check on this good man Mike who was trying to help me before you fucking hit him." I don't know why I'm even explaining myself.

"Jesus Christ. Let me fix this baby." He pleads, trying to pull me right back in. He brings his hands to my face and searches for more damage.

I shrug him off. "You done yet?"

"Done?"

"Done fuckin' every goddamn thing up?" I know my words are hurtful, but I'm just so fucking tired and done with it all. I can't keep letting him shit on me.

"I'll never be fuckin' done." No truer words have ever been spoken. He's never going to let me go. No matter how much it hurts him or me, he's gonna hang on 'till it kills one of us, maybe even both of us.

7
Lost

Tank

My head pounds, my body aches, and my mouth is dry as fuck. Rolling my head to the side, I know I'm in my bed at home without even opening my eyes because it smells like Lil. Sweet and sugary. Again I drank too goddamn much, but not enough to block out the shit I did last night. It's all there.

Cracking one heavy eye open, I see Lil next to me. She's lying on her back with one of her hands resting on my arm. The comforter is covering everything except for the one long tanned leg that's always thrown out to the side. A few smears of blood are on her tan skin and it makes my stomach roll. My teeth marks have ruined that smooth leg. Letting my eyes roam up her body, I find the same thing on her shoulder. I know exactly what I did last night. I did the same thing I do every time I get drunk, I fuck her.

Fuck her to punish her. I fuck her to punish myself. It's fucking sick.

Rolling over, I grab the half empty bottle of rum on the floor, hoping to kill the sick ache that's taking over. I throw the rum back like I'm dying of thirst, like it'll cure everything. World hunger, poverty, and my pathetic fucking life. I drink like it'll solve all the problems in the world. Shutting my eyes, I pray like fuck I wake up soon, where things are good again, where things aren't a total fuck up because of me. But it never works that way. I'm just not that goddamn lucky, so I lay back down only to pass out again.

I wake up the same as I did a few hours earlier, except I'm alone in bed. Getting up, I snatch up the bottle by my feet and pull on some sweats. Walking through the house, I drink and look for Lil. Letting the cool burn of alcohol seer its way down my throat, I drown everything. Every thought, feeling, and concern, I smother it with the liquor.

The kitchen door is open, leading onto the porch when I walk in. Passing the clock, I see it's two in the afternoon and Lil should be at work, but I know she's not because she's been missing a lot of work lately. Another thing I fuck up.

Walking onto the back porch, she's sitting in a chair with her feet propped up on the railing, staring off in the distance. My tee hangs off of her small frame and leaves a lot of leg exposed. I can see where she wiped the blood on her leg off, but the teeth marks remain and I have to look away. I don't know why I have to get so fucking rough with my baby. She doesn't deserve this shit.

Lennie is lying at the foot of the chair and watches me as I walk outside. George is on the seat next to her while she pets him with one hand, and the other hand is holding onto a bottle of Jack. Her face is lost and lifeless and it's then that I know she's giving up. I can see it and feel it before she even looks at me. I know before I see her eyes and hear the words. I know she doesn't have anything left to give me.

Looking up she says, "We need to talk. I can't ... no, I take

that back. I *won't* do this anymore." She says quietly. Her voice

lacks any of that strength I know she burns with. I know exactly

what she means, but still I have to ask.

"Do what Lil?" Some sick part of me wants to hear her say

it. I want to hear her say the words so I can feel vindicated

somehow and blame her. I want the pain of her giving up on me,

because I've given up on myself. I want a reason to be mad.

"You, me, the drinking, the smoking, all this fuckin' shit

you keep putting me through. All the blame you put on me as an

excuse for the way you act. I wish I could say there are more bad

times than good, but there are absolutely no good times. Fuck, I

can't even remember the last time we had a good day. This shit is

killin' me Tank," she whispers harshly.

Tipping her face to me, she gives me those heartbreaking,

beautiful brown eyes that are shiny with tears, tearing into my heart. I know I've broken her. I've broken us. I try to find

something to say, some small semblance of shit to fix this.

But my pride steps in. It won't let me feel bad for her

'cause it's her fault I go through this every day. If I'd never met

her ...

"So what? You can't do it? You're the fuckin' reason for

this whole goddamn mess." This shit isn't on her, but I can't shut

the fuck up. "You made me this way. I fuckin' love you, and that's

why we're here." If I could just let her go.

Turning those big dark eyes to me again, she stares at me

like she doesn't know me. Now those eyes are full of tears. Fuck,

she look defeated. She never cries and I know this is it. Now, I just

need her to finally see it and move the fuck on.

"We will never get past this and I'm not gonna force you to

see that if anyone has the right to pissed off and angry, it's me

you selfish piece of shit."

"Really? Bitch, don't you fucking see? You're the selfish one. I live every day, every fucking day with the fear I'll lose you. The fear I'll have to bury you. So don't tell me you can't do *this.* You're so goddamn self-centered that you can't see anyone else's pain."

As the words leave my mouth, I register the severity of them. I want to pull them back, but I'm not quick enough. I know they're cruel and they're wrong.

"I'm not gonna fight with you. I'm not gonna walk away either, but I won't be your punching bag anymore. I know you're goin' through somethin' and I wish you'd let me help, but I'm not gonna beg you to." She says with resolve, waving between the two of us. Her mind is made up. She means it. She means every goddamn word of what she's saying and she has every right, but my ego and the booze speak for me.

"Fuck you, Lil. You don't know shit 'bout what I'm goin' through." And it's because I'm too much of an asshole to let her in.

"You're right, I don't know what you're goin' through because you won't talk to me. I'm gonna stay somewhere else for a while. We need time apart." Standing up, she grabs the bottle and takes a healthy drink. When she's done, she hands it over to me.

"I love you. I always will, but I won't let you kill us both. For once since this shit's happened, I'm pickin' me." I watch her back as she walks away from me. She's leaving me.

My heart tells me that I'll never let her go, but my mind says fuck that bitch.

****

Sitting at the bar with my trusty bottle, I stare at the wall and think. Stare, think, and drink. Drink and drink some more. Lil's done with me. She's just gonna walk away? After every fucking thing she has put me through? Do I blame her for it? No. But do I hate her for it? Yes. I feel lost and pissed the fuck off.

I've no fucking idea how long I've been sitting here now and don't really care. Got nothin' at home for me, and I've got nowhere else to go. My ass is numb, my back is stiff, and I should eat, but I really just need to drink more. Yep, I need more fucking alcohol.

"Hand me that bottle, bitch," I snap at Red. Her hands find her hips and she gives me an annoyed glare. Bitch is copping attitude with the wrong asshole.

"Hey bitch! You forget your goddamn hearin' aid?" Flipping her hair dramatically, she grabs the bottle behind her and slides it to me.

"You're a real dick," she mumbles. Stupid ass.

"And you're a fuckin' whore, guess we're even, huh, bitch?" She just glares at me as she stomps off. Bye bitch.

I'm sitting alone at the bar when the new whore starts giving me the eye from across the room. She's hot. Tits and a pussy, that's pretty much all that counts anyway. No need to look at her face, she isn't Lil. Lil. Fuck that bitch.

Lifting my chin at her is all the acknowledgement she needs. These bitches don't need a second invitation. They wanna fuck and be someone's Old Lady. I'll fuck, but that's all this bitch is gettin' from me.

Gliding her way over to me, she smiles. "Hi I'm Diamond. We haven't been introduced yet." She says as she bites her lip. I get nothin', not a twitch, tingle, not a goddamn thing. This bitch does nothing for my dick, or me.

"What a clever name." She bats her eyelashes at me and giggles. That wasn't a compliment. Great, she's also one of the really dumb bitches.

"Hopin' we could go somewhere n' get to know each other." There's a classic pick up. Her lip biting and giggling didn't get my dick hard, so let's see what other tricks she's got in her arsenal to get me up.

My feet drag behind the giggling bottle blonde bitch as she leads me behind her. It's like my heart is trying to get my body to stop before I do something I'll regret. Somewhere in the back of my drunk mind, I know this is wrong. So fucking wrong. I know I really don't want this, but I can't fucking stop myself either. I need this. Anything to get this shit out of my head. I need her out of my system so fuck it, I'll try anything.

Pulling me down the back hall, she pushes me into a dark corner. Instantly she tries to kiss me. Before Lil, I didn't kiss these nasty bitches around here. After kissing Lil and her perfect mouth, there is no way in hell I'd kiss these bitches now.

"I don't fuckin' kiss you bitches. Don't talk and get on your knees."

She drops down without a fight. Easy, eager and all too willing to suck a strangers dick. It's sad really, but she can suck away like her life depends on it if it gets me off.

Running her hands up and down my thighs, she's smiling and moaning at me. Sad desperation is oozing out of her lost eyes when she looks up at me. In my sick and twisted mind, I tell myself these are the best kinds of women. Fuck the independent, strong-willed bitches. They're too much goddamn work.

These women are so easy. They'll do whatever the fuck I want them to do, just to be near me. She wants me the way I am. There's no attitude, no opinion, no fight, no attachment. You can use them and throw 'em away.

Running her hands to the waist of my jeans, she bites her lip again. Not sure if that's to be cute or a nervous habit, but it's not sexy on her. Her blonde hair is frizzy and messy while her clothes are hanging limply and rumpled on a body that needs to be fattened up. I'm not into fat bitches, but I want my bitch thick.

She better look like she can take a pounding. This girl is young and already broken. Bitch can't be over twenty-one. She doesn't have to tell me shit 'cause I already know she's lived a rough life. Bitches like this are easy to exploit.

Lil's seen a lot of shit and been through some hard times, but that girl has been well taken care of. This little blonde on her knees keeps glancing up at me for praise for every touch, but she's not getting it. The only bitch I praise hates me.

Her fingers find the button on my jeans like a fuckin' pro. She's a professional as she pulls it open and reaches a hand inside. Shit's so wrong it makes me cringe, and still, not a damn thing when she touches me. Her hand squeezes my dick and the unfamiliarity of her skin on mine makes me fucking sick. The guilt builds up 'till I can't fucking stand it. Fuck! I just want to forget. I want to get lost for just a few minutes. Lil fucks with me in the worst ways. She's not even here and she's still fucking with me.

Pulling away from the sad little blonde, her hand falls away from me and a flash of disappointment crawls over her face. She really wanted this. All these pathetic women in here are dying to be an Old Lady. If they only knew that it takes a special kind of bitch to be one. The brothers sense that shit the moment that type of bitch walks into a place, and they snatch that type of bitch up. These whores never had a chance. Nothing they do will make them Old Lady material. No amount of dick sucking or fucking will get them there. Even if they get made one, it won't last long.

"You ain't gettin' it done, *sweetheart*." I lay blame on her 'cause I don't want it. She just ain't her. She ain't Lil. No woman ever will be.

Fixing my jeans and walking away, I sit back down at the bar to drink some more. Drink and drown that shit out. The little blonde goes back to her seat and gives me her sad eyes, but I just ignore her.

"The fuck ya doin' drinkin' alone?" King asks as he sits down next to me.

Tryin' to forget Lil, tryin' to drink my life down the goddamn drain, and tryin' to block out the day. I'm tryin' to drink shit back to normal, or desperately try to kill myself. Pick a fucking answer.

"Why the fuck not?" I retort instead of laying all my shit down for him. What the fuck else would I be doing? Fixing shit in my life and with my woman? Yeah. Not happenin'.

"Lil's still bein' a bitch I take it." Normally he'd be on his ass for that comment, no one talks about her like that, especially someone like King. But right now, I couldn't agree more. The alcohol couldn't agree more.

"Yep." Filling up a shot, he holds it up to me.

"Here's to Lil! The bitch of all bitches." King yells out.

"Fuck that bitch." I scream.

"Fuck yeah! Drink up n' let's go ride." I think King might understand me after all.

8
Rampage

Lil

"You gonna be alright sis?" Gin asks from beside me on the bed. His back is leaned against the headboard, Peaches next to him. A tub of ice cream, some terrible, but oh so good Taco Bell with two bottles of wine, and a big ass bag of skittles sit on the bed with us. I'm drowning my sorrows in terrible food. My head is resting in Peaches lap as she mindlessly braids my hair. Anything to focus on other than Tank.

"Yeah, I think so." I lie. Since I left Tank's, me and my dogs have been crashing here. It's not home, but it's comfortable, and it's family.

"Want me to beat the sense back into that motherfucker? I could punch the stupid outta him too." He grumbles with his eyes still fixed on his video game. As sweet as that is, I think, I'd rather not hurt Tank any more than he already is. As much as I'd like to punch him myself, I doubt it'd do any good.

"So this is it then?" Peaches asks me softly, looking close to tears. I hope she doesn't start crying. I haven't cried yet and I have a feeling once I start, I'll never fucking stop.

Is this the end? God I fucking hope not. Since meeting Tank, I couldn't imagine my life without him in it. The idea is sickening and it sends me into a desperate panic. I will never just walk away from him, but I can't sit here and watch him kill himself. I'm not going to pretend that it's okay anymore. I can't. It's not fair to either of us. If he needs me, I'm here. If and when he wants to let me in, I'll be waiting, but I'll no longer support his shit. I don't have it in me to deal with his constant bullshit.

"I don't know." I tell her honestly. I'm not going to let him take me down with him.

****

Walking into the local community college library, I look for a head full of long, golden blonde hair. I needed out and away from anyone associated with Tank 'cause I couldn't handle any more of the pity and sad looks they were giving me. I appreciate everyone's love, but I had to get away. I came to see a friend who knows very little about my family.

Lailah is someone I've been tutoring. Not that the girl needs it. I swear sometimes she teaches me more then I teach her. She's damn smart. I guess she'd fallen behind in some classes due to personal issues and needs to catch back up quickly so she's able to finish the quarter with passing grades. The school board asked that she get some tutoring to make sure she stays on track. If she doesn't, she'll lose her financial aid and for her, I don't want that. I wish I could say helping Lailah is a chore, but it's not. She's so goddamn sweet and easy to be around, it actually feels like a relief. We've become close these last few months and she's really helped to distract me from Tank and the whole mess we're in.

Lailah's a good shoulder to lean on, a good listener, and she's easy to talk to.

She'd make a good sister I think idly. I could induct her into the Disciples Old Lady club. Maybe for Tags or Crush? Not that I'm an Old Lady any more. The thought rubs that painfully raw spot in my heart again. I'm not an Old Lady. I hadn't thought about it that way, but there'll be no more Tank and Lil if we can't fix this. We won't be a family like that anymore and that idea hurts and makes me panic, but I have to remember this is for the both of us. I can't continue to feed into the shit and act like everything is okay. I suck it up, hold my head high, and push those fucking tears away.

"Hey there, love bug!" Big blue eyes and a bright smile find me.

"Hey doll!"

Lailah and I get right to it. We spend two hours working nonstop. She writes and I tidy it up, but there's not much to fix.

She's smart as hell. Pushing back from the table, she throws her hands up in air and sighs.

"I'm done. If I look at that computer screen anymore, my eyeballs will explode."

"Right. I'm bored as hell 'cause you're not leaving me much to fix. You're too damn smart and already know what you're doing."

Rolling her eyes, she laughs.

"Sure. Sure. I'll screw up more so you'll have something to do."

"Thanks babe." Her face sobers and she gives me a soft smile.

"So how are things with your man? Things getting any better?" I give her the whole sad run down from start to finish. She listens and tries to offer some helpful advice.

I love my family more than anything. I love my girls too, but they are biased. The guys' answers to my problems are usually either something violent, or they tell me to suck it the fuck up. Peaches and Cali's advice is usually the same, but they add in that I should just leave his ass. Lailah's an unbiased opinion.

"It sounds like he loves you. I'm no doctor or anything, but it kind of sounds like some form of PTSD. He's stuck in the past, in that one moment. He's terrified something will happen to you, so he's pushing you away because in his mind, he won't have to deal with it if something bad happens to you if you're not around."

"You're too damn smart Lailah, but that's why I love ya."

"Just an outside opinion." Stuffing all of her stuff into her bag, she starts to laugh.

"Yeah, I'm smart with some things, and I'm clueless with others. It evens itself out. I've got to run to class so text me later honey. And for the record, I think things will work out. Patience is a virtue."

"Thanks smarty pants. Bye." Giving my cheek a quick kiss, she's off.

Cleaning up my stuff at the table, a kid from my last quarter's class plops down in Lailah's vacant seat.

"Hey, you got a second?" Damn Lailah for leaving me. I should have followed her out. This kid is a fucking pain.

"Yeah. What can I do for you?" I ask him, putting on my responsible and helpful big girl teacher panties. He begins pulling a wrinkled piece of paper out of his back pocket and he slaps it on the table, unfolds it, and points to a bunch of scribbles and chicken scratches. This should be interesting.

"Since I dropped your class last quarter, I had to take it again. I'm not understanding this paper on Mark Antony and his contributions. I know it's not your class anymore, but you got a sec to give me a few pointers?"

Thirty minutes later, I feel like I'm still stuck just explaining the directions and premise for the entire paper. Andrew is one of those students who got a free ride through school on an athletic scholarship. He's single minded and football driven. He means well, but if he spent half as much energy on his school work as he does on the field, he'd be fine, but he doesn't, so he's not. My phone starts to vibrate in my pocket and pulling it out, I see Tank's name flash across the screen.

"I'll be just a second, Andrew." He waves a hand at me and starts texting. That could be his other problem.

"Tank? Everything okay?" I wasn't expecting him to call me, so it makes me wonder.

"Where the fuck ya at?" Taking a deep breath, I go to answer but Andrew speaks up.

"So do you think I could add that shit about his childhood?"

"Who the fuck is that?" Tank growls into the phone.

Pulling the phone away from my ear, I tell Andrew, "Just give me a second please." Putting the phone back to my ear, I tell Tank, "Sorry. I'm at the library tutoring."

"Who the fucks the dude, Lilly?" Lilly? Instantly I feel defeated. He's trying to pick a fight. I'm not going to win no matter what I tell him. He could be a ninety-year old man who was comatose and Tank would still be crazy about it.

"Tank, stop. He's a student that asked for my help when I was on my way out."

"Yeah?" He questions me. He doesn't believe a word I'm saying. I've never given him a reason not to trust me, but I'm in no mood to argue with him.

"Yes Tank."

"Needed you, but since you're too fuckin' busy with *Andrew,* I'll let you *help* him."

"Tank..." is as far as I get before he disconnects the phone. My heart dips and my head sags. I want to throw my hands up and say "Fuck It!" Fuck. I give up.

After leaving the college, I find myself at the club. No clue why since Tank was a huge asshole on the phone, but here I am anyway, like the fucking doormat I've seem to become. It's a place I've been avoiding since having that talk with Tank three days ago. I haven't heard from him except for earlier, but I haven't seen him at all. It's not like I've called or looked for him. This divide is wearing on me. I miss him, and it feels so goddamn wrong to go this long without, at the very least, speaking to him. In the past he's gone on runs for a week or two, but we always talked. He's always been there in some way.

Sitting in my car, I stare at the door, debating whether or not to go in when Tank and King walk out the front door. For a long moment Tank stops and stares at me blankly. There is absolutely no emotion when he looks at me. I wonder if I should wave? Maybe I should get out and talk to him. Should I just ignore

him for being an asshat?

I wave and give him a little smile, because at the very

least, I want him to know I see him. As much as he pisses me off, I

never want him to feel like I don't care.

I don't have the chance to get out and talk to him 'cause

without so much as an acknowledgement, he gets on his bike. His

cut covered back is turned toward me as he slips on his aviators

and avoids me.

Cranking up his bike, he doesn't even look my way. A little

piece of my heart dies knowing he doesn't care enough to

acknowledge me. I showed up. I didn't have to, but I did.

Throwing my Jeep in reverse, I get the fuck out of there. I'm not

going to let him see how much he makes me hurt.

Walking into Gin and Peaches place, it's quiet and dark. I

hate it. They have a nice place that's homey and lived in, but it's

not my home. It's not Tanks place.

After taking a quick shower, I throw on some sweats and grab a glass of wine from the kitchen. Hell, I should just forgo the glass and just straight shot the bottle. Flopping back on the couch, I set about channel surfing. I watch mindless, terrible TV for a while, drink my wine and sulk.

A loud knock on the door a few hours later startles me, but before I can get up, the door opens with a loud bang and in stomps Rampages giant body. It never ceases to amaze me how fucking huge he is. He looks around and his eyes stop on me. Something along the lines of pity and anger stare back at me.

"What the fuck ya doin' in here in the dark, all by your damn self drinkin'? Throwin' a fuckin' pity party, is that it sis?" He asks me.

Holding up the remote, I tell him, "Channel surfing?".

This pity party only has room for one, but he plops down next to me and jerks the remote out of my hands as usual. Men and gadgets. Guess he wants an invite to my sad shindig.

"Not no more, sis," he says with a smirk. Flipping through the channels, he finally asks after hijacking the remote, "What do ya wanna watch?"

"I really don't care."

"Still lettin' that asshole get to ya, I see." He say's rolling his head toward me and giving me a lazy look. How could I not? He holds my heart in his hands and is currently using it for batting practice.

"I'm alright. I'm a survivor, and I'll survive this too."

"I know you'll fuckin' survive. But I know shits eatin' at ya."

"How do you know that?" I don't know why I ask because it's so obvious. I'm a sad ass mess.

"How long I known ya?" he asks plainly. We've known each other for so long.

"Since I was little."

"Yeah sis, I have. Know when somethin' is really botherin' you 'cause it's always in your eyes. Your mom was the same way. They were her tell. I can tell this shit's eatin' at ya. Ya gotta let it go, darlin'. Not a goddamn thing you can do 'bout it 'cause he's gonna have to want it for himself. He's not gonna do it for either of ya, so you have to accept it and move the fuck on."

"How?"

"I know that stupid motherfucker loves ya. Let him the fuck go Lil. Sooner or later, he'll figure it the fuck out, but don't let him take you on this ride with him. Ya don't deserve that. Ain't your shit to work through, it's his, n' he's the asshole who's gotta do it. Just move forward. Shove down all the negative n' go the fuck forward. Suck it up sis."

Suck it up? Yeah because I haven't been trying that. Rampage has always been in my life. Always in the background though, quietly watching. I know he has a bad temper and some fucked up shit goin' on in that head of his, but for all that temper and badass, there is a big heart in there. It just takes a lot of digging to find it. I know he's right, he usually is.

"But still don't get the whole "love" shit. Not worth no one's goddamn time." He grumbles.

"How'd you get so damn smart?" I counter.

Tapping himself on the forehead he says, "All that listenin' n' not talkin' I do. Learn a lot 'bout motherfuckers that way darlin'."

We hang out watching dumb shit for a while, so I decide to go get us some food. I'm standing in the kitchen making me and Rampage something to eat when I hear my phone ring.

"Will ya get that?" I call for Rampage. He's been silent since his advice, and I appreciate the silent company and support. He's always been good for that. A moment later he comes into the kitchen looking mildly annoyed.

Handing me my phone, he grumbles, "We gotta go.

Somethin' 'bout Tank bleedin' all over the fuckin' club floor."

9
Bleeding Like a Stuck Pig

Tank

My arm stings like a bitch. Nothing a little tequila and a blunt can't fix.

"You're going to need some stitches for that." The good doctor says, pushing his glasses back up his nose. I figured as much. Fuck, I'm bleeding like a stuck pig all over the place and I think I can see bone. King drug that damn dirt bike right the fuck over my arm, leaving a nasty slice.

"Well then, stitch it up doc."

"Would you like some medication for it?" Does he really fucking think he needs to ask me that?

"Fuck yes. The good shit."

A couple of pokes and I'm numb as a motherfucker. Too bad he couldn't do that shit to my heart.

"What the fuck ya do?" Stitch stares down at my arm as doc sews it up.

"King's a stupid asshole."

Throwing his head back, King laughs and raises his beer in some half-assed toast. Stitch shakes his head and walks away. Getting pretty fucking sick of all the looks and disapproving stares. Fucking assholes. They don't stop that shit, I'll be breaking faces real soon. Sitting at the bar with my arm on a towel, the doc starts the pulling and tugging, sewing my shit up as I start my drinking and smoking routine.

"Shit Tank, what happened?" My baby's voice asks all soft and sweet, just like I like it. I hear her from somewhere beside me. I'm numb, high and feeling fucking good. Somewhere deep down, I knew she'd come. She always does. Turning my head over on my rested arms I see her standing by me. She's leaning over the bar, staring at my arm. Fuck I've missed those eyes. The way

she's looking at me with sadness, love, and with her whole heart

has me feeling fucking desperate all of a sudden. I feel out of

control. I want her here. I don't' want her to ever fucking leave

me again.

"Aye baby, c'mere." I just want her close to me. Holding

my hand out to her, she steps toward me and right into me,

where I want her to be. I have no fucking clue what's gonna

happen tomorrow, no fucking clue if this is the last time I'll see

her, touch her, or even be near her again, so I have to have her.

Just can't let this shit go.

"Let's go."

"Tank," she says hesitantly. I watch her battle my request.

I know she doesn't really want to come with me, but her love for

me won't let her tell me no, and I'll use that against her to get my

fix, always hurting her to get what I need. If I was a good guy I wouldn't do this shit to her. I wouldn't ask her to do shit I know she doesn't want to, but I'm not a nice guy.

"Just want you Lil." She takes my hand and comes with me. No questions asked.

Pushing her body up against the bathroom door she molds right into me. Those legs go instantly around my waist, arms around my neck and fingers digging as I touch every square inch of her body. I run my hands over every sexy curve and feel every part of that perfect fucking body pressed against mine. Those big tits pressed against my chest, that sweet pussy rubbing against my dick. I am fucking crazy for her. I crave her like a fucking junky, and she's a habit I just can't kick.

Alcohol runs through my veins, pain meds numb my body, and the weed makes shit hazy, but I can still feel her. I'd know this body anywhere. I'll always know my baby's body.

"Why do you keep doin' this shit to me?" she asks in a pained whisper against my neck. I know I'm slowly killing her, but still she lets me. Fuck, I don't think I could even stop if I wanted to. Biting down on my skin, she licks her way up my neck. Shit makes me so goddamn hard, it's painful. This isn't to hurt her, this shit's all for me.

"Shut up baby. Just for tonight. Give it to me tonight." I know she will because she'd never tell me no. She loves me to goddamn much. And like a selfish prick, I take it from her. I'll keep on taking until there's nothing left of her for anyone else.

I don't do this shit nice. This is for me. Pushing that skirt to her hips and barely pulling my dick out of my pants I shove into her hard, so rough that her head hits the door. Pulling all the way out, I slam back into her tight, wet pussy so hard my balls slap against her ass. Her fingers are biting into my shoulders hard, her nails breaking skin. Her legs tighten around me as she holds onto me like her life depends on it. I fuck her hard, giving it to her rough and mean.

This shit is worth dying for, yet I don't even fuck her on the bed. I take it from her right here against the door of this dirty fucking bathroom like she's some club whore. I didn't even take her panties off, I just slipped them to the side and shoved into her. She's so fuckin' warm and wet, gripping the fuck out of my dick when I slide in and out. She's always so fuckin' tight that the shit makes my balls ache. I feel that wetness running down my dick and it's amazing. Even if she hates me, her body still craves mine. She might not want me, but I can still get her pussy wet.

"God fuckin' damn, Lil. Your pussy always wants me. You know no one but me will ever own this shit."

This shit is so fucked up. So good and so fucking sad. Pulling out fast, I slam back into her hard as she bites down on my lip. Tearing at my hair, pulling at my clothes, hurting what little skin she can find. She's trying to hurt me. There is no skin on skin. The only shit I can feel is that sweet pussy and it's not enough. She's trying to keep her body from me. I'll never fucking have enough of her.

"I hate you," she whispers around my lips.

"Baby yeah, I know you do." I fuck her like I hate her. I fuck her like I love her. I fuck her like it's the last time.

****

Fucking Lil last night just made things worse. I fucked her and let her walk away just like any bar bitch. She pulled that skirt back down and walked out the door, tears in her eyes and hate rolling off her in waves. She left without a goddamn word to me. Her hate is a potent thing, it's so goddamn thick it was almost palpable. I could feel it.

I know this shit fucks with her. I know she's confused. I know she's scared. I know she wants to get away from me. But I also know she'd do anything for me. I know she'll never be able to tell me no. As much as it kills me to hurt her like this, I can't help myself. I just can't fucking stop.

This last time was different 'cause it was for me. That shit wasn't for her. I treated her like gash, like some bitch not even worth any more time than it took to fuck her.

During times like this, when I lie down alone in this uncomfortable ass bed at the club, I wonder why I do this. Why I keep putting us both through this. I promise myself I'll fix shit; I'll get it together enough to get my woman back. I'll treat her the way I know she deserves.

Then I have one of those dreams, and all that shit blows up in my face. A few hours later, I'm right back to square one with her. I'm right back to drinking myself to death and trying desperately to get her the fuck out of my head and system, but feeling like shit for thinking about her that way.

****

It's been a week and I haven't seen or heard from her. She avoids me now and don't want shit to do with me. I hate not knowing what's going on with her. I know she's around 'cause my brothers keep me updated. It's not enough, but it keeps me from losing my fucking mind. The small updates and information about her keep me from starving.

I feel empty and lost without her and I'm fucking going insane. Fuck, I want so badly to go back to before that night. I want to forget all the fucked up shit I saw. I want the dreams and guilt to go the fuck away.

I try to focus my attention on the club instead of Lil, working to figure out all the legal shit for Low. I try to keep every fuckin' thing together for my brothers, but all that shit requires me to be sober. When I'm sober, I think of Lil. When I think about Lil, shit goes downhill real quick. So I drink, and when I drink, I can't focus on my club. I'm stuck in this vicious cycle I can't get out of. It's eating me alive and slowly but surely, it will kill me and I'll probably take her right along with me. No matter what I fuckin' do, we keep crashing and burning. I'm just waiting until the crash is too bad to come back from.

****

I'm sitting at the bar, where I spend most of my time now, when I hear her laughter drifting in through the door. I miss that sweet ass smile when she used to look at me like I'm the only asshole on the planet for her. I miss the way she lights up for me. I miss her laugh. Miss the way she loves me. I miss it all.

"Oh please, shut the fuck up. I didn't butcher it that bad." she giggles. It's my favorite fucking sound, until I hear Rampages deep gruff laugh with hers.

"Whatever ya fuckin' say Sis."

In they walk together. Lil's smiling over at Rampage as he's laughing down at her. Shit slices into me. She's not looking at him like she used to look at me, but she's still looking at him with something close to love, and that look is nothing like the ones she gives me now. I get nothing but disappointment and disgust.

Things start to get a little hazy and I know I'm about to flip my shit. I'll kill them both. I don't want to, but I will.

"Lil! Get the fuck in the office now!" Her big brown eyes swing in my direction. She looks a little surprised to see me, but there's no guilt there. Deep down I know she wouldn't do that shit. She's loyal to a fault, but still I can't stop myself.

"Tank … "

"Get in the fuckin' office." She doesn't flinch. She doesn't even bat an eye as she shakes her head sadly and gives me those heartbreaking eyes, turns around and walks out the door. She really just walked the fuck away from me. That's a fuckin' first.

Turning my attention to Rampage, I feel the rage work its way up and the need to break something has me on edge. He says one wrong thing, I'm breaking his motherfucking neck.

"You fuckin' Lil?" I throw at him. His eyes widen and he gapes at me. Yeah the motherfucker actually looks shocked, but it doesn't last long. Rampage is not an asshole you fuck with. You bring shit to him, you better be ready to take it right back. He's one of the only people I try to avoid throwing shit at, but right now I just don't give a fuck.

"You're shittin' me, right?" he asks lamely.

"Sure the fuck ain't. What the fuck was that shit?" I nod at the door Lil just walked through.

"You drunk?" He throws back. I ignore his little dig.

"You looked pretty fuckin' cozy n' friendly with Lil." Even to myself I sound crazy. I've got crazy pouring out of me.

"Well, you look pretty fuckin' stupid," he counters without a second thought.

"Fuck you." All kinds of crazy shit runs through my head and I just let that shit spill out everywhere. It's like once I start, I can't stop.

"You finally lose your goddamn mind?" he asks calmly.

"Sure the fuck haven't. You tryin' to fuck my Old Lady?" He actually laughs. Throws his head back and laughs at my question. I don't let him laugh long. Planting my fist into his chin, he shuts up real quick. Done laughing so fast?

"Imma let ya have that one, *brother*. Here's some education for your stupid ass." He growls at me, shoving his hands into his pockets, probably trying to keep himself from beating me to death.

"Ain't tryin' to fuck with Lil. She's been like a sister to me since long before your ass came along fuckin' shit up, so don't bring your shit to me. I'm helpin' her out. She needed shit moved from your place, so like real family does, I helped her. If your head wasn't so far up your motherfuckin' ass, you'd figure it out." Rampage doesn't speak much, but when he does he doesn't hold shit in.

This shit is all news to me. He helped her move her shit? She really is fucking done with me. She moved out? She wasn't supposed to go this far. She's supposed to fucking stay so I know she's still mine, whether she want to be or not.

"None of this shit would be goin' on if you'd act like a man. Suggest you pull your shit together before you fuck it all up because believe me when I say she's ready to leave your ass for good. N' when she does, there won't be a goddamn thing you can do 'bout it because she won't be your *Old Lady* any goddamn more."

****

It's all gone. When I walked into the house it didn't feel the same. The air is cold and quiet, empty and fucking sad. Every goddamn thing is gone. She took it all except for a pair of boots by the side door. Seeing that shit makes me feel fucking crazy. She left the house shit, but took all her shit. All the important stuff is gone. That last nail in my coffin is the house key sitting on the kitchen counter. This is it. That shit ripped my heart out and let the bastard bleed all over the fucking floor. I couldn't be in that house any more. I wanna burn it to the ground. Strike a match and let that motherfucker burn. It's not a place I want to be without her. Nothing left in my heart anymore but hate. I hate that bitch. I hate that I loved her. I hate that I don't have her in my house and in my life anymore. She finally came to her senses and I am pissed.

****

I have nothing left, so fuck it. I give up. Grabbing a couple of bottles of Cognac, Tanqueray, Jack, some X, coke and Trix, I head straight to hell.

10
Road Rage

Lil

I had to get my things out of that house. We need space and that's what I'm giving us. We need miles of it. Maybe it'll bring us back together in the end. You know the saying, absence makes the heart grow fonder? God, I fucking hope there's some truth in that. If not, then I don't know what I'll do ...

The thought of being apart hurts, but I have to do it. Then again, maybe this shit is all for nothing. Maybe there is nothing more that can be done. Right now I'm choosing to have hope though. I'm choosing to hang on to what we used to have. I'll protect it with my life. I'll do whatever it takes. My last ditch effort is giving us space, distance and time.

I'm trying to be patient and understanding, but he makes it really fucking hard. All I know is that we've got to get along and deal with one another. This club is my life too, so we have to find some balance and be civil. If leaving is what can wake him up, I'll do it. I'm trying to bring him back to me. He may push me away from himself, but I won't let him push me away from my family. He will not run me off.

****

Not surprisingly, the club is pretty busy today. When I pulled in, Stitch and Rampage were acting like they were twelve and beating the shit out of each other in that godforsaken ring while Gin's hunched over his bike, tinkering away. Everyone is working and it's business as usual around here. Walking into the club, the air shifts and something feels off as soon I step through the door. It's stifling inside. The relaxed vibe from outside is nowhere to be found on the inside. Happy makes a bee line for me before I can make it past the front door.

"Whatcha doin' here sis?" Is he serious?

"Uh, is that a trick question?"

"Sure the fuck isn't. You wanna grab up some lunch with me?" He asks. His voice is a little panicked and his eyes are a little frazzled. What the fuck? Since when does he want to hang out with me? Lately he avoids me like an ex-wife.

"Yeah, after I've done a little work ... What the hell is wrong with you Happy?"

Waving me off, he says "Nothin'." He's being pretty dismissive while he glances around. Yeah, I'm not believing him.

"Seriously, why are you acting like a fuckin' nut job?"

"Damn, I'm not. You wanna go for a ride with me then?" Okay, that's it. Something's goin' on. Either that, or he got into some bad weed.

"Alright. Well I got shit to do so I'm gonna let you stand here and act weird, my friend." Side stepping him, I make a grab for the office door.

"Lil, please," Happy clips in an agonized groan, but it's too late, the damage is already done. Biggest mistake of my life.

My breath leaves me in a rush as my lungs compress painfully in my chest. I feel like all the air has been violently punched out of my body and my poor damaged heart stops and burns in my chest as I struggle to get sufficient air into my lungs. My vision blurs and those fucking tears find their way to the surface.

My desk is a fucking mess. All the papers I had neatly stacked on top of it are strewn all over the floor. My eyes follow the trail of empty bottles of liquor and discarded articles of clothing littering my office floor. That terrible raw spot in my heart splits open and bleeds slowly 'cause nothing in my life will ever be as terrible as this.

Tank is sprawled on the couch in the corner, wearing only his black boxer briefs. One arm is thrown carelessly over his face, while the other is hanging off the couch, clutching a bottle of Tanqueray, and blood from his newly stitched up arm is dried to his forearm. Trix is completely naked, lying on top of him. Her body is molded to his, and I can see some sick satisfaction on her face even in her sleep. I swallow down the vile lump in my throat at the sight in front of me. I want to scream. I want to kick the fucking shit out of the both of them, but nothing happens.

I feel completely numb, like this is an out of body experience. It's like I'm watching it happen to someone else. My mind won't let me process the scene in front of me and I blink back the tears, willing them away. I'm not doing this. Not here, not now. Taking a deep breath, I turn around to leave. Out of nowhere, the whole goddamn club is watching my epic downfall and humiliation. They're all watching me, faces expressionless as they stare at me. I will not cry. I will not fucking cry. He's not worth my tears.

"I've gotta go." I whisper through the choked back sob and tears.

"Sis," Gin pleads softly, grabbing my arm as I pass and I can see the pity in his eyes. Why would Tank do this? They all probably saw it coming. I can't do this. I *will not* do this and I shake his hand off me.

"Leave me the fuck alone." I can't look at him. I can't look at any of them. I turn and walk out of the door.

****

"Hey Sammy. Any plans for the next few weeks?" I sniffle into the phone pathetically. God! I sound like a soppy ass loser, but I'm all cried out now, leaving me a snotty and raspy mess. I finally let it happen and I let all that shit go. I couldn't hold it in once it got started, so one tear was followed by a million. I cried for a while. I cried until my eyes felt swollen and raw and there were no more tears left. Now the tears have dried up and morphed into to something different.

They've turned into an emotion I can't place and if I could, I wouldn't even have a name for it. It's something like love mixed with hate, and a little bit of rage thrown in. I want to say it's hate that they've turned into, but I don't think I could ever truly hate him. No matter how bad I want to, I just don't think I have it in me.

I feel so betrayed and let down by my best fucking friend. He was always supposed to be on my side, treat me good, and to love me. He was never supposed to break me like this. I should have never let him in. I should have never trusted him. The sad part is I'd do it all over again to be able to feel that intense love for the short time I got it.

The worst part of this whole mess is I feel fucking stupid. How could I have not seen this coming? I feel like I left that door wide open for him, like I invited the trouble in. As much as I want to blame Trix for this, it isn't her fault either. She was doing what she does 'cause she's a whore. That's all she'll ever be 'cause it's all the bitch knows. She knew Tank was mine, but she did what

I'm sure he asked her to do. I hate the nasty slut, but it still isn't her fault. But when I see her, I'm still gonna kill her. I'm going to kill them both.

I've gone through the, *what ifs*. What if I would have tried harder? What if I would have loved him more?

Fuck that. I did everything that I could have done and I refuse to take the blame for this anymore. He acts like he's the only motherfucker that had to deal with this shit. I had to be strong for him, but he couldn't, no, wouldn't give that to me.

With the phone pressed to my ear and my face pressed into my pillow, I whine to my cousin.

"Shit baby. My schedule just cleared so pack a really big bag. I'll let Trace and Tyler know you're headed our way. Daddy will clear out the spare room for you."

"Thank you." I sound like I'm having an allergy attack.

"Don't thank me, but let me know who the dead asshole is that Daddy's gonna be ordering a hit on."

****

On my five hour drive I listened to every sad song ever made. *I'll Be, Nobody Knows, Nothing Compares to You, Foolish, It Will Rain, Have You Ever, Tears in Heaven* and the list goes on. I listened to them on repeat while I sobbed, letting my fifteen dollar mascara run down my face. I stopped by every comfort food drive-thru I saw. I stopped at Krispy Kreme, where I ate five glazed doughnuts and stuck the other seven in my back seat for later. Wendy's, there I ate a large fry, deluxe burger and nuggets. Baskin Robbins, I got a triple chocolate cone and a gallon to go. Don't judge me. Heartbreak does this to a girl.

My sad self-pity grew into violence. I got mad and beat the living shit out of my steering wheel. Fuck him. Fuck him for breaking my heart. So I listened to every angry girl power balled out there. *You Oughta Know, Don't Take It Personal, Take a Bow,*

Creep, Fancy, Hit Me With Your Best Shot. My four personal

favorites were, *Smoke, Drink, Break-up, Just Like A Pill, Alive,* and

Teary Eyed. They all left me feeling empowered and ready to drag

that asshole behind my Jeep by a long rope on a sharp rocked,

gravel road, with some razor blades thrown in for shits and

giggles.

Then I proceeded to have a bit of road rage, taking my

anger for Tank out on my fellow travelers. I cut off a bitch in a

station wagon, I threw my ice cream cone at a man on a bike,

flipped off a trucker, and break checked a douche in a big truck.

I'm not proud, but feelin' slightly better. It was a long trip, but I

made it in one piece, and with part of my sanity.

****

My Uncle Danny's club looks nothing like ours back home.

Where ours is very industrial with metal, concrete, steel, and

exposed duct work, theirs is rustic, worn and woodsy with wood

of every kind, river rock, and natural colors. Their club is basically a tiny broke down cabin in the middle of the woods on a river.

Old. It's up in the mountains of Oregon, off a logging road that

winds its way through the mountain side. If you were a hiker and

stumbled upon it, you'd definitely think some axe murders

happened here. I packed up my Jeep and headed out here as soon

as I got the go ahead from my Uncle. Not that I needed to pack

really, my shit was already in bags, which is sad all on its own. I'm

fucking homeless. I'm a homeless, manless, makeup smeared, hot

mess. Sad days.

I turned down that long gravel logging road and was met

by my cousin Tyler and two other guys. I guess they were

expecting me to bring people with me. Even though they are a

chapter of the Disciples in Washington and they've always been

close, these guys out here in Oregon are a little reclusive and

guarded when it comes to anyone not directly in their club.

I've spent time up here during the summers playing in the

rivers and lakes with my cousins. We'd run around this place,

camp out, fish, raft, drive the back roads, and play on ATV's.

During the winter, on the rare occasion the club wasn't safe, my dad would send me and my mom up here too. We'd play in the snow and sled, sit by the fire and play games. Even though this isn't home, it's pretty goddamn close. I feel comfortable and safe here.

I'm safe from Tank here.

For all that this place lacks in esthetics, it makes up for in memories and heart. This cabin was my Uncle and Mom's great-grandfathers years ago. Over the years, it's been added on to and fixed up with minimal repairs, but it's held strong. This place has strong bones so I can see why my Uncle picked this place to call home.

"C'mere Sis." my Uncle waves me over as soon as I set foot out of my Jeep. All the way over here, the nickname has carried. Since I was a little girl, it's been what the guys have called me. I guess being like their little sister, it just kind of stuck. Either way, it doesn't bother me anymore. It is what it is and there's no changing it now.

"Thanks for lettin' me crash." I tell him as he pulls me into a bear hug, squeezing the air out of me.

"Don't thank me for shit. You're family n' we do for family, always. Anyway, I send your ass away, Lucy will haunt my ass." He says as a sad look passes over his rough and wrinkly face with the mention of my mom, *his* little sister.

"Well I'm happy to be here." Hearing him talk about my mom hurts, hitting that slowly healing part of my heart reserved for her. It's healing, but part of me thinks it'll never fully recover. What I wouldn't give to have her here right now. A shoulder to cry on, a source of never ending support, and a back bone made of love and steel that would have been here to help hold me up. She might have even killed Tank for me. God, I miss her.

"Here." Taking my bag from my hand, Dan hurls it to a man standing a few feet away. "Take her shit up to her room."

The man catches it. Nodding at Dan, he looks at me and gives me

a chin lift and a soft smile.

"Lilly."

Buck. A man I've known a long time. I used to spend

summers here and he would occasionally stop through our place

when we were younger. We used to be pretty close. His light

brown hair is shaggy and messy, standing on end and it makes me

smile. That man has perpetual bed head. Where Tank is

handsome and rugged, but beautiful, Buck is rough and hard, very

much a mountain man. A face covered in a full beard hides a good

portion of his face. Both arms are sleeved from fingers to

shoulders, his chest and back completely covered in colorful

tattoos in every variety. Hell, they run to his thighs and they run

up this neck and to his chin.

We had our little thing when I was seventeen and he was

eighteen. It was a few weeks of summer fun. It was during a time

Josh was fucking around on me and I'd broken it off. He got his and I got mine. Buck and I are good now, we always have been. He got married and had a few kids while I moved and went to school. Friends are all we'll ever be and I'm good with that.

"Hey Buck. How are you?"

"You're sad babe." He says completely ignoring my question.

"Nah, I'll be good."

"Let me know who I need to kill, alright," he says and chuckles.

"Yeah, well, I think I want him alive as much as I'd like to kick him in the balls. I'd rather not have to bury him. Kinda love the fuckin' asshole."

"Alright. I'll hang back, but say the word n' he's a goner."

Sammy makes her grand entrance as I walk toward the living room. Of course like everyone, I stop and stare at her. Her long, silky light blonde hair sways and shines in the light as she glides her way toward me. I swear she practices that walk. The beauty queen even waves as she walks into the room with a tight white dress on and some Jackie O shades on her head. All she needs is a yappy small dog in her arms. She seriously kills me. Born and raised in the same life and we couldn't be any more different, but somehow, we work. She's the sister I never had.

"Babe." She says softly, pulling me to her. "What the hell is wrong with that man?" She asks me. There's that badassness.

"You're wearin' a virginal white dress with the mouth of a sailor. Very classy, Sam." She throws her head back and laughs.

"Fuck you. Let's get drunk and bitch about men."

Sounds like the kinda party I need.

****

Sitting in the living room of the house, we drink and chat. The guys have all but disappeared. As Buck had said, "Your annoyin' ass woman yappin' is scary. Imma be in the garage. If ya need me, find me."

They all cleared out as soon as we broke out the wine. I had a glass or two, but I'm not in the mood to get drunk and wallow in my Tank pity. Alcohol only makes it worse.

"So you know everything?" I'm still a little surprised, and pissed off that the news of me and Tank traveled all the way down here. Damn. It's like a game of phone between these clubs. News travels fast.

"Tags kept me up to date. I mean, he's shit at givin' detail, but I pieced it all together." Wait. Wait. I was not expecting to hear that name out if her mouth.

"Tags? You talk to Tags? Like, on the phone? Disciples Tags? My Tags?"

She shrugs and starts chugging her wine. Oh yeah, keep trying to keep that mouth busy. Sooner or later, you'll run out of wine. She can't drop that shit and not explain.

"Care to give details?"

"We're friends." Oh that's not good enough.

"And? When did y'all become friends?" Not that I don't find that amazing. Tags is such a good guy. He deserves a good woman.

"Well, I mean we've known of each other for a while. I came up there to visit and we talked. We started talking the night of your welcome home barbeque. He stops through sometimes, n' we text n' shit."

This is all news to me. Tag's talks on the phone and texts? Not sure why, but I find that crazy and funny.

"Holy shit. He fuckin' you too?" Well that got a blush out of her. The dirty little skank-a-roo. "I want details."

By this time, Sammy is smashed. I stopped drinking after two glasses 'cause shit was making me emotional. I do not need to be drunk dialing Tank. She's spilling all kinds of dirt though. Drunk Sam is fun Sam.

"It's huge Lil. Like two handfuls, girth." Not what I wanted to hear. I wanted light details, not the gruesome ones.

"Imma stop ya right there. Details I do not need to hear." She giggles and holds her hands out dramatically.

"*Two* handfuls. You know how amazing that is?" Yeah I know. I had one of those back home. Even during girl time, Tank invades my thoughts. Damn him.

Lying in my adopted bed for the night, everything feels wrong. I'm a few hundred miles away from Tank, but he's right here with me. He's all I can think about. The good, the bad, and the ugly are all there making me miss him. No matter what I do, he's there. Love fucking sucks.

11
Arsenic

Tank

"Knew I should have beat the fuck outta you when Low gave the order." Gin paces back and forth in the corner while cracking his knuckles, glaring at me. "You were in charge. Low left this shit for you to handle and you said you got it. You were supposed to keep shit on the outside goin'. I've been handlin' as much shit as I can, but can't do it all." He growls at me. Fuck him and his *order*. Fuck Low too.

"Lost us a deal, lost us a fuck ton of money. You let that little fucker get a piece of the shipment 'cause you were fucking slippin' *brother*. You've been too fucked up to see It. You cost us, but I decided to let it go 'cause with the shit you've been putting Lil through, didn't wanna put more shit on her by fuckin' you up.

But not now. No fuckin' way I'm lettin' that shit slide now, not after what you did to my *sister*."

He's right, I let that little fucker get away with stealing from us, but what the fuck ever. I'll get that piece of shit one way or another.

"Stand the fuck up," Gin growls down at me. Blood is dripping from his mouth as he stares me down with pure hatred. He's brimming with contained rage as he waits for me to get back up and throw fists.

Pushing off the couch, I get back up, wipe the blood from my mouth and face the asshole head on. I can feel blood still pooling in my mouth and if that fucker knocked a tooth out, I'm gonna kill him. I will rip his goddamn head off.

Spitting on the ground by his feet, I see nothing but blood on the ground, but no teeth. Fuck it, I smile at him. Why not have a little fun? Low ordered this and I might as well take it. I'm trying my fucking hardest not to fight back and let him have this because this isn't just for shits and giggles, this is a goddamn order, but it took me truly fucking over Lil to get it from Gin. He held off, but there's no fucking way around it now. I gave Gin one to the mouth when he started to get a little too personal for my taste. He wants to do this shit over his issues with me and the club, fine. Lil is off fucking limits.

Shit isn't in my DNA to take a hit and not hit back, but I know I've got this shit comin'. I deserve it tenfold. Fuck, if Low was here, I'd probably be in a body bag halfway to the morgue already. This is how we handle shit around here. There is no chatting about our feelings. We communicate with our fists. Fuck it's hard to hold back when he's beating the fuck out of my face though.

"Took her mom dying and Low needing her to get her the fuck back home, took ya 'a fuckin' year to make her leave us."

That one stung like a bitch as he puts his fist into my nose. Shaking my head, I try to push the sting away. I stumble back a little, my eyes water instantly and I'm pretty fucking sure the asshole broke my fucking nose because it swells instantly. I wipe the blood away and face him again.

"Fuck you."

"At the club? In the goddamn office that Lil works in? You fucked all this shit up when she showed up and fuckin' saw you asshole. Saw that dead bitch Trix laid up on you, and now that whore's blood is on you. You broke our girls heart n' now imma break your goddamn face."

I took it from Happy and Gin. They both laid into me good while Stitch and Tiny watched with happy as fuck smiles on their goddamn faces. Happy and Gin got a little of it back, but I took that shit because I deserved it.

Cracking his knuckles, Rampage smirks at me from his silent post by the door. "My turn, motherfucker."

****

Lying on the bed at the club, every fucking thing about me hurts. My face is fucked up. I'm pretty fucking sure Gin broke my nose, blacked my eye, and spread the bruises around. He fucked up my right cheek too. Happy busted up my lip and left a nice fist sized lump and bruise on my stomach. Oh but Rampage had the most fun. I think he broke my jaw. The fucking asshole laid into me good. If Gin didn't break my nose, Rampage sure the fuck did. I think he broke a few ribs and if he didn't break 'em, he sure the fuck cracked 'em. I'm bruised from head to toe. Shit aches so goddamn bad, but it's my heart that hurts the worst.

I fucked shit up so bad I don't think I could ever get Lil to come back from it. This shit is so much worse than when I left her alone at my place. I broke something in her that'll never be fixed. And if it could be fixed, I wouldn't have the slightest idea where to start. I can't even fix my goddamn self. I hate that this is where we are and I hate that I caused all this damage and hurt. I should pack up my shit and go nomad for a while, give everyone a fuckin' break.

"Why'd you fuckin' do it asshole?" Peaches screams at me, pointing wildly. "Haven't you fucked her over enough? Why'd you hurt her like this?"

"None of your fuckin' business, bitch." I snap at her. Cali is standing in my doorway, watching quietly while Peaches is behind her making all kinds of noise, trying to push her way in here. If she can make it, I'm gonna smack the fuck out of her.

"None of my business?" Peaches repeats slowly.

"You stupid? You fuckin' heard me."

Charging at the door, Peaches looks ready to kill me. Cali braces her arm on the other side of the doorway to stop Peaches. I don't know why I'm eggin' her on. I shouldn't even bother. Jesus Christ, I don't want to hear it from her. I already got it from the guys, I don't need her shit too.

"Fuck you! You're fuckin' disgusting. I can't believe you fucked that nasty piece of gash over Lil."

Her words make my gut twist painfully. When I fuck up, I fuck up so goddamn bad. Sadly I don't even know what I did or didn't do last night. I was so goddamn fucked up I can't remember anything past seeing Lil's key on my kitchen counter. That was it for me. I might have fucked that stupid bitch; I might not have. God, I was so fucking high I'm not even sure I could have gotten it up if I wanted to. I'm so fucking stupid. I should have fought harder. I should have never let that shit go. Part of me wants to tell Peaches I might not have fucked that gash, but what's the point? They saw that bitch naked on me and that shit didn't look good. They're not gonna believe me anyway. Fuck it.

"I hate you!" She screams at me. Yeah bitch? Well I hate me enough for the both of us.

****

"Here, asshole." Cali says sitting down next to me on my bed a while later. No knock, nothing. She just came right in, making herself comfortable as she leans against the headboard, pushing me over. Rolling over to look at her she looks shocked and a little squeamish when she sees my face.

"Oh fuck. Yeah, you're really gonna need these." Holding her hand out to me, she hands me four white pills and a shot. I lift, or at least try to, an enquiring eye at her.

"It's the good stuff honey," she assures me. Fuck it. I throw the shit back and chase it with the liquor.

"Why you here Cali?"

She shrugs her shoulders and looks like she's thinking about it. "Not really sure since I fuckin' hate ya n' the fact you ran our sister off, but I know Lil would hate to see you like this n' I love her, so here I am taking care of her man because he's too much of a fuckin' mess to do it himself." That one stung.

"Thanks." I tell her sarcastically. I may be fucked up, but I didn't miss her little jabs. She's not in here for me. This shits all for Lil.

"Don't thank me. If I had it my way, those would've been somethin' to kill your ass. Considerin' Lil loves you n' so do your brothers, I settled on two drugs instead, but don't get it twisted. You don't fix this shit with Lil n' get her ass back home to us, it'll be some Arsenic in your meatloaf next time." She says and smiles sweetly at me. No clue how Stitch puts up with her scary ass.

"Sorry I fucked shit up." I give her my half-assed apology. No clue why I'm telling her sorry. It wasn't her heart I broke. Cali isn't the woman I fucked over.

She shakes her head and says, "No, you're not. If you were sorry, you wouldn't have kept doin' it to her." Alright then, whatever.

"Not gonna argue with you Cali." Again she shakes her head.

"I know your fuckin' not, but what you're gonna do is pull it together n' fix it. It's your job."

"Yeah?" I challenge her, even though I'd rather grab up my bottle and drown my problems instead of sit here and bullshit with Cali.

"Yeah Tank. You're a fuckin' man. You fix shit n' hold it down, it's your goddamn job. That shit that happened with Lil was bad. She almost died on you, but she almost died on us too." I go to say something but she stops me with a hand in my face. "Shut up. You're gonna listen to me." Damn this bitch is annoying.

"That shit that night was as bad as it gets, but it's your job as Lil's man to be strong for her, not the other way around. She's the one who went through being tortured, beaten and shot, not you. Yet, she was taking care of you and making excuses for your sorry ass 'cause you cant' let people help you. You ever stop to think with all the shit from that night, the shit with her mom, and the shit with Low now, that she may need your ass? Your Old Lady, your Lil may need someone to lean on? Maybe she needs someone to be strong for her? She's been through all this shit, and she's the one who's been handlin' your stupid ass. I hope you feel less than a man, because you are. Everyone sees you this way now and you should feel ashamed that it was your woman who should've had you to help her through it, not you havin' your woman takin' care of you." Well Fuck.

How many times have I tried to think of ways to move past this? I'm so goddamn selfish I didn't even think about it that way. She's so fucking strong, I never thought she'd need me. Again I go to say something, but she shuts me right up.

"You shut your fuckin' mouth, square your shoulders n' buck the fuck up for her when she needs you. If you're gettin' stressed 'bout it, or shit is botherin' you, you bring that shit to your brothers. You know they'll help you. Don't put that shit on her. She's lost so much already, almost lost her life, so can't you stop your own fuckin' pity party to see that? Don't let your shit fuck her up any more than it already has. She loves you. You love her. So what the fuck is the problem? You have to prepare yourself for the fact that Lil will die someday." I don't wanna hear that kind of shit.

"Don't say that fucked up shit to me."

"Shut up Tank." She glares at me. I decide to shut up so she'll hurry and get out of my room. "Lil will die. It's life. We all will, but sittin' 'round, constantly thinkin' about it ain't livin'. Wasn't your fault Josh was crazy. Not a goddamn one of us saw that comin'. Shit happened, but you can't live everyday worried she'll die. Life ain't worth livin' if you're gonna live it like that. Love her n' enjoy her while you've got her Tank. If you hadn't fucked it all up, you would've had your forever with her. She loved you like that. You have to wanna do it for yourself, but please, for Lil, you need to fix this. She deserves that much." She deserves so much more than that.

****

A few weeks later ...

So I've pulled my fucking shit together, sort of. I still drink because it helps fill the void that was created when Lil left me, and I still have the fucking dreams. I stay at the club 'cause goin' home without her isn't an option. I don't sleep at night, don't eat often … hell, I don't do a whole lot of anything, but I have pulled it together enough to keep this fucking club going. I keep it together enough to not completely fuck it all up with my brothers. I keep it together enough so that if and when Lil decides to come back home to me, there will be something for her to come home to. Everything that Cali said hit home. Out of all the shit she spewed at me, I got it. I need to hold shit down. For me and Lil, I need to work this shit out because I've decided I will not live without her.

"You ready?" I ask Blade, giving a chin lift towards the cracked and peeling front door. No window, no peephole. This motherfucker has no idea we're outside. Nodding his head, he goes for the porch of the old run down house we're at. Taking cautious steps, he makes sure to keep his eyes on the door. We've got his back. It's rainy and wet outside, but the heavy pounding of the rain helps to drown out any noise.

I hug the wall, letting the roof overhang keep me as dry as possible. Stitch cocks his head toward me to the side, then he nods over, around the corner and holds up his hand. He signals there are two guys on that side. Looking at Rampage, he holds up one finger. One guy on his side. Four of them, six of us. Blade does a quick sweep of the porch and nods me forward. Kicking in the front door, I hold it open with my foot and I nod for him to go in ahead of me.

This is the asshole that I let slip and he stole from us. You steal from us, you're not only stealing from my club and brothers, but you're stealing from my family. Stealing from our Old Ladies and our kids. Fuck that shit. I may have missed what he did, but we're here to get it back. You don't have our money? I'll be taking something worth value. Whether that be your car, your fucking house, or your life, I'll get back what you took from me.

Walking inside the run down crack house, we split up and start looking. I know I'm not going to find the money, but who the fuck knows what else I'll find. These trap houses are always filled with all kinds of goodies like drugs, weapons, and other stolen shit. The house is filled with filth, that's for sure. Fucking gross. This shithole makes the club look like a goddamn castle. I dig and tear shit up; break this and that and rip shit apart. I could ask the guy, but you know that motherfucker isn't going to give up shit, at least not yet. Plus, it's kind of fun to give him time to try and think up something sneaky and creative to tell me about where my money magically went.

"Tank," Blade calls for me.

Walking down the hall, I find what I came looking for. Blade has the little thief on his knees in the middle of kitchen, gun to his temple. Sad part for him, his little partners aren't in here to take some of the blame, so he'll get it all. This part is the fun part though. I like to taunt and scare them. I like to fill them with false hope and ideas of life and all that grandeur. Let him think shit is good and then surprise, you're dead.

"Didn't think I'd come lookin' for you, did you asshole?" I ask him.

The man starts to shake violently, pleading with me in broken sobs. He pretty much offers me everything, including his first born to let him live, but he doesn't offer what I came for. Never understood why people act so damn scared when we show up looking for what ya took from *us*. You're stupid enough to fuck with us, then you shouldn't be scared when we come looking for ya. You know what you're gonna get when you deal with us.

"Sorry man. I'm fuckin' sorry." The bitch sobs. "I got half the money."

"Sorry man. Half ain't the number I'm lookin' for. I bet you can do better than that."

****

We cleaned up our mess and got what we came for so I head back to the club. I haven't been home since Lil left and I won't go back there 'till she's back, so the club is where I'm staying now. It's been a few weeks and I haven't heard from her. I fucking hate it. The only people who have are Gin and Peaches, but I don't bother asking about her anymore 'cause they won't tell me shit. It bothers me. It eats at me. All Peaches said was she's good and I have to be okay with that, 'cause that's all I'm getting. I pray every fucking day she's somewhere safe and someone is keeping an eye on her. Every day is a struggle, but I'm trying. Fuck I'm trying.

I miss her so goddamn much it makes me sick. It's hard to function without her here. She's all I fucking think about and I can't seem to see past her. This is what I wanted, wasn't it? To have her out of my life so I wouldn't worry about her every second of the day?

I'm starting to see there isn't a life beyond Lil for me. She's the only goddamn person on this planet I want. After Lil left my ass, Cali's hateful but heartfelt lecture, along with the vote around the table for me to step down if I can't pull my shit together, I had to choose. I had to fix shit in my life. I had to get better for Lil, the club, and myself. I've decided I'm not gonna lose Lil or this club. I won't live without either of them. I'm suckin' shit up and I'm pulling myself together. I'm trying to move the fuck forward, but I need my fucking woman back. If I want to get her back, I have to get better. I need to work on moving past the nightmares and live in the here and now. I can't change the past, so I have to work on the future.

Out of the corner of my eye, I see the red and blue flashing lights approaching quickly. Fuck. Just what I fuckin' need. Pulling over, I know I'm about to face a shit storm. I've been running from this for a while now. The officer gets out of his car and heads straight for me with his cocky walk. Stuffing his glasses into the front pocket of his uniform, he bends over slightly to look right at my face.

"Evenin', Roman." The cop nods his head at me. I can see the little gleam of accomplishment there in his eyes. He's been waiting for this for a while. Fuckin' asshole.

"Sheriff." I nod back.

Giving me a once over and then looking over at the guys, he looks back over to me. He's outnumbered, but it's not like one of us are gonna kill him, but he doesn't know that. No one is trying to spend life in prison right now.

"You've got a warrant out for your arrest, Roman. Remember that assault you skipped out on?"

"That guy survived I take it then?" The officer stiffens and gives me a hard stare. He doesn't look like he enjoyed my little joke.

"I've been looking for you for a while now." Knew that was coming. "I've got to take you in."

No point in fightin' him. If I'm gonna take care of this shit, now would be the time. I look at Gin and give him a chin lift. He knows. He returns it and pulls off. They'll come back for my bike.

"Alright. Looks like we'll be spendin' some time together then, huh Sheriff?"

"Turn the bike off and put your hands behind your back, Roman."

"Sure, as long as I can ride shotgun on the way to county."

12
Positive

Lil

"Holy fuckin' shit. Read it again." I shake my head holding the offensive little life changer away from me. "I think I'm gonna be sick." My stomach rolls, and a cold sweat dots my brow. I feel faint. Why? Why? Why? Someone somewhere hates me. Like, really fucking hates me.

"Girl, you throw up, I'll throw up." Peaches warns me from the bathroom counter.

"Try another one, doll." Lailah encourages softly from beside me. She's rubbing small circles on my back, trying to comfort me, but it's not working and I'm still freaking the fuck out. Cali is going through plastic bags and tearing open boxes like a mad woman.

"You fuckin' try one." I tell Peaches.

"Babe, already did. It's all you." Yeah I'm going to throw up. Sticking my head back into the toilet, I dry heave some more. My stomach squeezes and my body shakes. Why?

"This can't be happening." I groan into the toilet.

"It'll be okay. We'll figure it out." Those are some famous last words if I've ever heard any. I think I just need to lay down.

The four of us lay on Peaches giant bed. I lie down and listen to them tell me how things will be okay, we'll figure it out. They make plans and figure things out for me. We work through point A to Z. I can't see past that stupid blue line. Oh fuck I think I might throw up again. I can't be pregnant. I haven't had sex in months.

"I'm like, almost three months pregnant." I damn near cry. Now I want to throw up again.

I haven't seen or spoken with Tank in a few months. I haven't heard anything about him either. No one brings him up and everyone avoids the topic of us. Everyone just stopped talking about him completely around me.

I think about him constantly. I miss him so much. It's like I'm missing the most important part of myself. Everything I do makes me think of him. I stayed away from home for almost a month, but it didn't do a goddamn thing to help. I still fucking missed him, even though I still kinda hate him.

I stayed at my Uncles for three weeks after I left. It helped a little. It helped to be around new faces and a different scenery. Sammy, Trace, Tyler, and the guys kept me occupied and busy. I then spent a week with Cali and Peaches in the city. We did some major retail therapy. We ate expensive food at some of the best restaurants in the city, we pampered ourselves with various, highly priced, spa treatments. That too kept me distracted, but it was only momentarily. My happiness was short lived and in sporadic intervals at best. No matter what I did, Tank was always there in the back of my mind. I wish things could have been different.

When I got back into town, I rented a town house in town, about thirty minutes from the club. I needed to start putting shit back together and keep my life moving forward. As much as it killed me to do this without Tank, I had to for my own sanity. I couldn't give up, so I picked up a few classes at the college and continued tutoring Lailah. I spent some much needed time with my girls. Gin comes by and usually brings one of the guys with him so I visit with them that way and they bring any important paperwork I need to keep up with club shit. I talk to my dad every few days and I visit when I can. I left the club that day and I haven't been back since. Right now, I don't think I could ever go back there, in that office, even if I wanted to.

"We should make you an appointment." Lailah says softly as I stare at the wall.

"You really think you're that far along? Is it? ... Oh Jesus." Peaches asks me. She almost looks like she might be sick too. Oh fuck me.

"Seriously Peaches? I haven't had sex with anyone but Tank, and yeah, it's been that fuckin' long." What the fuck was she thinking with such a stupid fucking question.

"Well fuck," Peaches grumbles. Cali actually looks excited. If I wasn't having an emotional breakdown, I'd slap that sappy look right off her face.

"What the fuck am I gonna do about Tank?"

****

The doctors words echo in my head. They just float around in my numb mind, around more numbness. This cannot be real.

"You are most definitely pregnant. I'd say almost eleven weeks. Congratulations." She said with an elated smile. To my doctor, this is fantastic news. Shit couldn't be better news to her. To me? Not so much. For me this is life altering news; Life changing shit. Eleven weeks. Eleven fucking weeks. How the fuck did I let this happen? God we weren't even having sex regularly.

We're not even good. We haven't spoken in forever. What the hell am I going to do?

I sat in the parking lot of the doctors office for three hours Googling all things baby related. Labor, Braxton Hicks, stretch marks, diaper rash cream, cord blood, car seats, amniotic fluid, colic, all words I've heard, but never given much thought to before now. Now I'm neck deep in everything baby and I think I might be sick again and I feel a panic attack coming on. There's a baby inside of me. I'm going to be a mom. My baby is growing in there. It has legs and arms, it has hair, and it even moves around in there. Holy fucking shit, there's a baby in there.

The last few weeks I've been tired and not feeling so great, but I chalked all that up to stress. Shit hasn't been easy these past few months, but I would have never pinned it on a baby until Peaches put that shit in my head. She filled my head with worry until I gave in and peed on that stick. And fuck, she was right.

Laying my hand on my stomach, I let it sink in. That's my little baby in there. I tell myself that I will figure this out. Whatever it is, I'll push through it, just like I always do. We'll be okay 'cause I'll take care of us, but I've gotta tell Tank. No matter what's happened, he should know. It's only right. Whether he wants it or not, I'm keeping it and I'll take care of my little person.

****

Sitting at the club, I stare at Stitch like he's lost his fucking mind because I'm really starting to think he has. They all have. He's being so goddamn evasive it isn't even funny.

"So you have no idea where he is?" I let the baby news sink in for a few days before I decided Tank needed to know. I called him. I called for three days to no avail. I went by his place, I waited at his place, but I got nothing. I left a note on his door, but still got nothing. I was starting to think he was avoiding me so I tried the only place I knew he'd be, the club. So here I am like a fucking loser, hitting up everyone, looking for my baby daddy.

"No sis. Told ya I don't." I find that hard to believe. He's the fucking acting President. No one seems to know shit about him. He's disappeared, just like that nasty gash bitch Trix? Coincidence? I don't fucking think so.

"When's the last time you saw him then? What about his nasty slut Trix?" He shrugs his shoulders and looks away as he starts picking at the label on his beer bottle.

"A shrug ain't gonna work with me Stitch." I want to tell Stitch it's important, but he'll ask why and I can't tell him yet.

"Don't worry 'bout her anymore babe. Bitch won't be back. She got *handled*." I don't push for more on Trix. He said she was handled, then she was handled. Plus, I really don't give a fuck about her. I have bigger and more important things to deal with right now.

"You really got no fuckin' clue where he is?"

"Why?" he counters. "You need somethin', I'll help."

I can't tell him, although I want to. It's bad enough Peaches, Cali, and Lailah know before Tank. A part of me feels it's only fair he knows before *everyone* else.

"I just need to talk to him. How longs it been since you've seen him?" I try everything and I've asked everyone.

"A while," he says shortly. A while? That's pretty fucking vague. I know that's all he's going to give me. Fuck.

"Whatever. If you talk to him, will you please tell him to find me?"

Kissing my forehead, he looks a little skeptical but says, "Sure thing sis."

****

"Imma tell you where he is, only 'cause I fuckin' hate seeing this shit." Rampage growls from the couch, looking uncomfortable as I cry. He's sitting as far away from me as possible without it being completely obvious. He won't look at me and he looks antsy. It's been two weeks and I can't reach Tank. He's nowhere. I tried everyone and no one would be straight with me. I'm always getting the run around and no ones stories match up. If and when I can get some sort of answer from someone, they're always half-assed and a bunch of bullshit. I feel like I'm losing my mind.

Finally I called Rampage in tears. I'd run out of options and people. He was my last hope. And no matter what, Rampage is always straight with me.

"Please, I'm fuckin' desperate. Like a fuckin' loser, I've tried everything and no one will help me." Giving me a small smile, he nods gruffly.

"He's in county babe. Been in there for a few months now." My heart stops. I feel all that stuffed down anger float to the surface. He's in jail? He's been there this whole fucking time, all while I stress and worry. I'm sitting here crying like a mess and he's in county.

He's in jail and no one thought I should know? Not a goddamn one of them thought to tell me? He never thought to tell me? What the fuck is wrong with everyone?

"What the fuck did he do?" Shaking his head, he looks me in the eyes and says, "Ya know I can't tell ya that babe. Club business. He wants to tell ya, then that's his business." Suddenly telling Tank about the baby doesn't seem like a good idea.

"Why the fuck wouldn't anyone tell me?"

"He didn't want you to know." Rampage says sadly. He didn't want me to know? "Why?" He shakes his head and shrugs his shoulder.

"Don't know sis."

So like an idiot, I still tried to reach out to him ... again. I don't know, probably because I'm a glutton for punishment or I could just be desperately stupid. I'm overwhelmed with the thought of having a baby. I don't need him to like it, I just need him to know it, so he can decide if he wants to be a part of my baby's life and I can prepare myself for his answer.

At first I tried to send letters, but they'd be sent back unopened. I tried to call, but he won't speak with me. I even went and visited to only be turned away. He wouldn't even see me. I wanted to tell him about the baby even after he didn't tell me he was in county. I still thought he should know.

Not now. Now I don't care if he knows or not. He doesn't care enough about me to even tell me that he was in jail. He won't even see me, take my calls, open my letters, so fuck him. I guess he's finally got what he wanted; rid of me. I'm okay with that so fuck him. He doesn't deserve to have me or *my* baby in his life.

So I was sad, and then I was mad, maybe a little sad and mad again before I got reasonable. I had to stop thinking with my heart and emotions and start thinking with my head. I thought long and hard about it. I agonized for so many sleepless nights over it. I've looked at the negative and positive, and I've looked at all sides. I think its best right now if Tank doesn't know about the baby. With all the shit he went through, and now the whole jail thing, I don't need that in my life. I don't need it in my baby's life. Call it selfish, inconsiderate, or whatever you want, but I've got to think about my baby. I can't have all that bad shit in our lives right now, or ever. I need to focus on my baby and me. I'll tell Tank at some point. I won't keep the baby from him, but I also have the responsibly to keep my child safe, happy, and healthy, and right now I don't think Tank can contribute to that, especially with my sanity. He has too much shit to work through. He needs to fix himself before meeting my baby.

13
Bars

Tank

This place is depressing as fuck. It's sad and lonely and I'm stuck in this tiny ass, six-by-eight foot brick walled room for twenty-two hours a day. I see day light one hour a fucking day, the other is spent in general population. The bed is terrible with its thin mattress and one blanket. It fucking blows. The food's disgusting. I try not to go crazy in here, but it's pretty hard. I'm too fucking big for a room this size. I feel caged. Fuck, I *am* caged. Not a goddamn thing to do in here but workout, read, and think.

I'm alone in here. The corrections officer said, and I quote, "Roman is a risk to room with other prisoners with his gang affiliations." Guess I'm a fucking gang member now. Don't remember joining a gang, but I'm good with not sharing a room so it's a win/win. It's not like I'm going to go crazy and start a riot or kill everyone, but I'd rather do my time alone than with some asshole I don't fucking like. I prefer the solitude to the drama of a celly anyway.

I spend all day thinking about Lil in this tiny ass room. She's all I think about while stuck in hell. God, I'd kill to be out of here and with her. A few weeks ago I heard she was looking for me. That shit made this place worse knowing she was out there needing me and I'm stuck in this fucking place. There's not a goddamn thing I can do for her in here and I fucking hate it.

She'd sent me letters and I couldn't bring myself to open them. She called too. I don't deserve that shit right now. I don't know if I could handle reading or hearing her voice yet. That shit's like a drug to me. One taste and I'll need more. Best to cut it cold turkey.

She came by here and I couldn't see her. It would fucking kill me, eat me alive to be able to see her and not fucking touch her. That's my girl and I'll be goddamned if someone tells me to keep my hands off her. I can't bring myself to see my baby while in here. I also don't want her to see me like this. She doesn't need this shit on top of all the other shit I put on her. This is my mess and I'm dealing with it.

I fucking miss her. I miss her like nothing I've ever missed before, but one week and I'm out of this fucking place and I'll be working hard as fuck to get my woman back. While I'm in here, I let shit settle and I work on ways to fix shit once I'm home. I work on pulling myself together enough to get Lil back home with me.

****

Flicking my headlights off, I duck down in my seat. Sitting in my truck around the corner, I'm stalking these motherfuckers like some dumb fuck. I'm tired of the bullshit, tall tales everyone's been feeding me since I got home.

Been out for three days and all I can get are shoulder shrugs and stories from everyone. No one seems to know where my girl is. I find it hard to believe she was here looking for me and now she's magically gone when I come back. I know one of those motherfuckers know where she is. If they think they can hide her from me, then they are fucking crazy.

No one's gonna give it up, so I'm gonna find it out for myself. They underestimate my ability to find shit out. I'm like a goddamn detective, so I followed Gin and Rampage. I want my baby back and I'll do what the fuck ever it's gonna take. I'm not going down without a fight this time. She better come out swinging if she wants me to back off.

My two asshole brothers pull out of a complex of town houses in town, both of them splitting off in opposite directions. No fucking clue what or who is in this place, but I've seen Peaches, Cali, and the two morons come and go from here. These motherfuckers wouldn't all be coming to the same place for nothin'. There's only one person who'd bring the club in like that. Lil.

Hopping out of my truck, I walk toward the place. I left my bike at the club 'cause I'm not trying to get caught being a fuckin' creep. I didn't spend two days working this shit out to only have my bike get my ass caught.

They've all been coming from the one on the end. It's the place with the white front door and flowers on the porch. I feel like a fucking psycho doing this sort of shit, but I've gotta know. I'll do what the fuck ever it takes. Lil was looking for me, so she must need something. I need to know what it was now that I'm out.

Walking down the sidewalk, I work my way through the complex. It's dark and cold outside tonight. The only light is coming from the street lamps above. Walking up the steps to the front door, I pull my gun. I have no clue what I'll find inside so better to be prepared than to be shot.

Squatting down, I pick the lock. Thirty seconds and I'm in. That lock was a fucking joke. I find out this is Lil's place with a lock like that, I'm gonna beat the fuck outta Gin for letting her stay in a place with a lock that took thirty seconds to break into.

Pushing the front door open, the lights are killed. It's silent and dark inside. Looking around I don't see anything, nothing that even looks familiar. I walk through a living room with a kitchen attached and I don't see shit that says Lil. The place is void of any personal items and the furnishings are sparse.

The first floor is empty. Hitting the stairs, I head up to the second floor. Walking lightly, trying to be quiet, I look through open doors into empty rooms. A light on at the end of the hall has my attention. Walking to the end of the hall, I look around the corner. What I find stops me dead in my tracks. I feel like the breath has been kicked the fuck out of me.

Fuck I've missed her. I've missed her so goddamn much it hurts just to look at her.

Three raised scars on her tan back, that long, soft dark hair is wet and pulled over her shoulder. I follow that smooth back down to the curve of her ass to the tattoo I want to lick. Jesus Christ, I missed her. I'd know her from anyone. She doesn't even have to look at me, I know that's my woman. I feel her all the way down to my bones, and they fucking ache for her. The need is almost too much to handle. I take a few steps into the room, needing to be closer to her.

"Lil." She jumps and spins around, an arm covering her naked tits. Her eyes are huge when she looks at me. I want to look into her eyes, but I can't. Holy fuck. Holy fucking shit. Breathe. Breathe. I remind myself to breathe. In and out, deep breathes.

It's been months since I've seen her naked body. It's been so goddamn long. I can't stop staring. I'm stuck. So fucking stuck.

"Tank," she clips. "What the fuck are you doing here?" I feel fucking dizzy. I need to sit down. Yeah sitting down might be good. Backing up a few steps, my legs find the bed and my ass finds a seat.

No fucking way. *No* fucking way. She catches my eyes and turns around quickly hiding herself from me. For a long moment I try to put shit together. I try to make sense of it all.

"Turn back around Lil." She doesn't say anything and she sure the fuck doesn't turn around.

"Look at me." I demand harshly. She sighs deeply and with an annoyed groan and an arm securely covering her tits, she turns back around slowly. Her eyes are narrowed now, her mouth tight and pissed. In those eyes, she's nervous and unsure. Her other hand is rested on her stomach protectively, shielding it. A tiny rounded stomach.

"You're …. *Fuck* … You're fucking *pregnant*?" I choke out. I choke on the words. I choke and forget to breathe.

****

I'm now sitting on a stool in her kitchen, staring at her stomach. I'm not even fucking sure how I got down here in the first place. So I stare, because I've no clue what else to do. I asked if she was pregnant and she gave me an obvious eye roll and marched that ass right on past me. Now I'm stuck here in a house that does not, in any way, say Lil, while sitting on an uncomfortable ass stool, trying figure this shit out. A million questions fly around in my head, but nothing is coming out of my mouth. Pretty sure I've opened and closed it six or seven times, but each time I choke.

Nothing makes sense. I watch her move. I watch her body, her face and those fucking eyes for something to point me in the right direction, but she avoids me. She's fucking pregnant. My girl is going to have a baby. She's gonna be a fucking mom. I'm finding this all fucking crazy and hard to swallow. Opening up a cabinet, I see a row of neatly lined bottles. *Bottles*. Not beer bottle or wine bottles. Fucking baby bottles. Suddenly I find my voice. All my shit just starts flowing out.

"Why didn't you fuckin' tell me?"

Turning around slowly, she looks at me like I've just asked her that shit in Spanish.

"Why?" She repeats slowly her mouth turned down.

"You heard me. You tryin' to keep that shit from me?" A look of utter hatred flashes across her face as soon as the words leave my mouth. She visibly flinches. Too late, it was the wrong thing to say. With a quick jerk of her hand, she slams a plate down on the kitchen counter, and she comes out swinging. The plate crashes on the counter, breaking into pieces all around her, but she's clutching that broken plate in her shaky hands like it's her last hope, as if her life depends on it.

"I fuckin' tried! How the fuck would I have told you? You were gone." She yells at me. Her eyes are wild and her face so goddamn hurt and angry it burns all the way to my *soul.*

Taking a ragged breath, she shakes her head and I watch her reel it back in. She stands there silent, pulling herself together.

"I tried. You wouldn't see me or talk to me." Her voice cracks and she chokes on a sob. I have to take a deep breath to calm down. I'm watching her heart break and that shit breaks me, but I need to know. I need to know what the fuck she was gonna do about this *baby*.

"Shoulda told a brother. They would have got the message to me. I shoulda known this shit, baby."

She scoffs, snorting a humorless laugh. Her eyes are so goddamn sad and broken, that full of life look to them is gone.

"You don't fuckin' get it."

"Wanna try me Lil? If I never showed up here, were you ever gonna tell me?"

"You really think I wouldn't tell you? Fuck. You really think that little of me? I didn't want everyone to know before you. I wanted to be the one to tell you. I wanted to share that shit with you. Not one of guys while you were sittin' in a fuckin' cell. It's *our* baby, not theirs. I wanted you to hear this from me. Jesus Christ!"

"Lil, is that my baby?" I ask the one fucking question eating away at me. I know she said *our* baby, but it doesn't register with me.

She looks fucking shocked. Another choked sob escapes her lips and tears well up in her eyes. Again, wrong fucking question. I'm a dumb motherfucker.

I know it's my baby. I just need to hear her say it. I *want* to hear her say it.

"It's *my* baby." She forces out. Picking up another plate, she smashes that one too. All of her hate for me is evident in her body, in the way she looks at me, and in how she talks to me. I broke her. I fucking broke the only person I have ever loved. I broke my girl.

"Get out." She whispers.

"Lil, baby," I can't leave here with her looking at me like that. We've got shit to figure out.

"Out!" She points to the door. Her chest is heaving and her finger's shaking.

"Fuck that shit Lil. Not leavin'."

"Get the fuck out!" She screams at me with tears running down her face. Picking up a cup, she hurls it right past my head. Hitting the wall it explodes, pieces of glass flying everywhere. I fucked shit up so goddamn bad …

****

Space. Lots and lots of fucking space, that's what I'm giving her. If that's what she needs, she's getting it. She wants that shit, she can have it. I'll give it to her in spades. She wants support, fine. She wants some money, okay. She needs me, I'm right here. I'll do whatever the fuck she wants. I'm just trying my fucking hardest to get shit back to right with her. I have to fix shit for her and this baby.

That baby. My baby. *Our* baby. It's the craziest notion. We're going to be parents. The moment you hear it, or in my case, see that your girl is pregnant, an array of emotions goes through you. From one end to the spectrum to the other, there isn't a fucking emotion you don't feel. And it's a fucking shit show. I'm living the fucking shit show.

The first act of the emotional shit show is *Denial*. There is no fucking way I'm going to be a dad. I have twelve plus years of fucking various women under my belt and not once in that time have I heard the words, "I'm pregnant." I can't get anyone pregnant. That shit doesn't happen to me. That baby isn't mine, but you keep that shit to yourself. Of course nine times out of ten, she's not lying and that baby is sure as shit yours. I spent that first twenty-four hours high as a kite, locked in my room.

The second emotion is probably *Blame*. Something along the lines of "the bitch is lying" probably crosses your mind. The bitch did this on purpose to trap me. She didn't take her pill, poked holes in the condom, or seduced me. Either way, it's your goddamn fault 'cause you didn't ask or do shit to stop it. You fucked that girl and you remember every amazing fucking second of it. Of course you usually don't verbalize these thoughts either, unless you're looking to have your dick removed, then maybe you're stupid enough to say it out loud. In my case, she wasn't lying, she had clear proof.

The third emotion is pure, unadulterated *Fear*. It's the scared shitless kind of fear. Damn near want to cry fear, pack your shit and run for the hills fear. I can't be a dad. I've got too much other shit to do, to see. How can I fit a baby into my life? I've got too much partying going on for this shit, too many beers to drink, too many blunts to smoke, and too much riding to do, in my case. Basically, a baby will cramp the fuck out of your style, and your life will never be the same.

The fourth emotion in your shit show is *Guilt*. This is a big one. This is when you've finally accepted that you're going to be a dad. Your baby is coming one way or another, and there ain't a damn thing you can do about it now. This usually happens when you see that positive test, when you hear the doctor confirm it, see an ultrasound, hear a heartbeat, or in my case, see the physical evidence on your girl. You start feeling guilty for all the bad shit you were thinking before you knew for sure. You feel bad for thinking the girl that's having your baby is dirty enough to cheat. You feel like shit for blaming her when you were right there fucking her, condom be damned. You feel bad for wishing the baby away. You feel like shit for the bad things you did before she said baby.

All the drugs and alcohol you've consumed, worried you'll pass that shit on to your baby. You're feeling bad for all the nasty bitches before his or her mom. All your bad habits start to weigh heavy on you. You feel guilty that you're a shit guy and how in the fuck am *I* supposed to raise a productive member of society when I'm one of the biggest fuck ups in it? I know nothing about kids, let alone little crying babies. You worry about how you'll support a child, and not just financially, but emotionally. You worry about your parenting abilities. That's a pretty scary step on the shit show line up.

So far, I've gone through them all. Right now, I'm finally able to say and think the word baby without wanting a drink. I'm going to be fucking dad ...

****

It's been two weeks and shit's running smoothly with my brothers. A few lines on some blow secured, also got some other shit locked down. In talks with patching in some new brothers and I got a better lawyer for Low. Shit is finally falling into place with my club. I've just gotta get my baby back.

****

Walking into the kitchen at the club, I walk in on something that makes me smile and it also hits a spot in me that hurts so fucking bad it makes it hard to see straight. Lil finally started coming back around. Shit makes me happy to see her, even if she won't look at me or talk to me. At least I know she's okay and I get to be around her. I don't deserve it, but at the very least, I get to see her.

Walking in, she's leaning against the counter, smiling and laughing softly. She's wearing a tight pink tee that shows off that tiny ass stomach of hers. If I hadn't spent endless hours all over that body, I wouldn't have noticed that stomach. But I have and I see it. Her face is lit up and happy, just like I like it. Miss that shit. Miss is so fucking much.

Peaches is leaning into her, touching her stomach while they both talk quietly to each other. That shit should be me. That's my girl and my baby. I should be the one loving the both of them.

Looking up at me, they both stop smiling. Those happy faces slip into ones of scathing hate. Lil hates me and Peaches definitely still hates me. I hate that she looks at me like that now. I hate that she still doesn't want anything to do with me.

14
Confessions

Lil

How did we get here? How the fuck did I let things go this far? He went from being my best friend and the most important person in my life to a fuckin' stranger. He's turned into someone I want out of my life and at the same time I want to throw myself at. How did we end up standing in a room together staring like we don't know each other? It hurts to be this distant. This is the second time I've seen Tank since the night I lost my shit. I pretty much had an emotional melt down in my kitchen. Everything had just built up, and seeing him had made it all boil over, especially asking such a dumb fucking question. I went crazy pregnant girl on his ass. I feel good and bad about it.

Walking into the kitchen, he leans himself against the counter and stares at me. Those beautiful blue eyes are sad and haunted. Part of me wants to ignore him, tell him to get the fuck

out of here and leave me the hell alone. A bigger, sadder, part of

me wants to throw myself at him and cry like a giant ass baby.

"Can we talk?" He asks cautiously. There's an emotion on

his face that I've never seen before; uncertainty. He's always been

confident and sure of himself. Always bossy to the point of cocky.

The man in front of me is anything but.

"Yeah."

Sitting at the butcher block island, he leans against it

across from me, careful to keep a safe distance. I'm not sure if I

should be thankful for that or heartbroken that he's finally

understanding that as much as I want him near me, I don't need

it.

"Gotta tell ya some shit baby."

"I thought *we* were gonna be talkin'?"

He asks can we talk, yet he says he's got to tell me shit. Figures it'll be him doing the talking. Giving me that smirk I loved to hate, he shrugs.

"Okay so imma talk, you're gonna listen, then you can talk if ya want to." Bossy fucking asshole. Some things never change.

Waving my hand for him to go on, he sighs heavily. Straightening his shoulders, he looks me in the eyes, takes a deep breath and prepares for war.

Giving me a look he says, "Please let me say this shit. I gotta get it out."

"Fine. Talk."

"I'm sorry baby. So fuckin' sorry. I fucked shit up n' I let you down babe. I broke somethin' in you I can never fix n' I hate myself for that shit. I did some shit I'm not proud of. I hurt you n' I'm not gonna say I didn't mean to, because that's exactly what I was tryin' to do. I was hurtin' n' wanted everyone around me to be as miserable as I was. I just never meant for this shit to get here though. I let shit go too far. I broke your trust n' your heart, that wasn't something I was tryin' to do. For that shit, I am sorry."

I listen to him talk. His deep, rough voice is softer then I have ever heard it. It makes my heart hurt for him. He looks lost.

"I love you Lil. I really fuckin' do. I'll always fuckin' love you." When he says he loves me the tears start to well up.

"Shit just ain't the same without you baby. Treatin' you the way I did was fucked up. I shoulda never taken my shit out on you. If I could, I'd take all that shit back."

God I wish it could all be taken back, but it can't and we both have to live with it.

"I don't expect you to forgive me. I don't expect you to take me back. I just hope you'll let me be a part of you n' the baby's lives somehow. I just wanna know you both. Whatever time you'll give me, I'll take it. So please don't shut me out of that little part of your life. *Please*. I don't wanna miss anything."

Oh God, my heart cracks. That painfully raw spot aches and burns with his words.

"I'll leave you alone babe. As much as it'll kill me, I'll let you live your life. I really will. You need me, I'm here. I'll always be here for you. Whatever, whenever baby."

"Okay." Is all I can manage to choke out before it turns into a full blown sob. My eyes sting with unshed tears as my heart aches and beats wildly in my chest. Giving me a soft smile he nods down at my stomach, his eyes are on my hand. My hand is rested there on my small bump. Something I've noticed I do often now that's just become habit. I don't even think about it anymore. I guess it helps me to feel close to my baby.

Before I can answer him, Tank takes three large steps toward me and reaches his large rough hand out toward me. Placing it lightly on my stomach, he smiles and laughs softly. This is the first time he's touched the baby. It's a painful thing for me to watch; A sad moment. This should be a happy time. This should be out of love and not guilt. For a moment he just stares with a smile on those lips and an easiness in his eyes. He looks me over and takes it all in. Looking up at me nods approvingly.

"Shit looks good on you baby. You make it look fuckin' perfect."

****

There are four of them here this time. Last time I came, there was only one. I could handle one. I can't do four of them right now. Holding hands, smiling, rubbing bellies, I can't fucking handle the cute couples. The sweet families, they make me sick. The guy directly in front of me won't keep his hands off his wife. Want to know how I know it's his wife? Because she's wearing a three carat ring, while he's got a gold band on. Oh, and when she says jump, he asks, "How high?" Pussy. Instantly I hate them.

I want that. That should be me. I don't want to be alone here. I want Tank here with me. After our "little talk", I miss Tank more than ever. It fucking sucks because I'm not ready to let him back in or forgive him. He can't have my heart back 'cause the fucking asshole doesn't deserve it. I want to hang on to that hate. I need it.

I desperately want to go back. Back before that night fucked up everything. Every once in a while, I catch myself feeling bad for killing Josh, but not anymore. I won't allow myself to feel sorry for that piece of shit. He fucking ruined my life, twice. He fucked everything up for me. He took away Tank, my chance at a fucking family, something I deserve. I just want my life back.

The office door opens and the receptionist with the overly painted pouty lips calls me back. I stuff my sad ass thoughts down and stand up.

"Miss Cruz, come on back."

****

I see Tank almost every day now. These past few weeks I've noticed a change in him. I haven't seen him drink. He's been completely focused on the club and work. He checks in on me daily, but gives me my space. It's always a quick and kind, "You alright? You need anything?" I see the old Tank coming back and I so desperately want that. Since our talk, I'm creeping up on eighteen weeks now, and things are slowly going back to normal. My heart still hurts every night when I go home alone to a place that doesn't feel like home and crawl into that bed that's missing Tank. I hate waking up alone and cold. Nothing feels right without him, yet slowly life is going back to normal, even if it's alone.

Two nights ago, I felt my baby move for the first time and it was amazing. It was just a small flutter, but I felt it right where my hand was resting while lying in bed. I cried myself to sleep that night. I cried because I was so fucking mad and hurt that Tank wasn't there to share it with me. Mad that he pushed me so much that we ended up here. It was only a little kick I could feel on the inside, but it would have been nice to have him there to tell him about it. I wanted to share that kind of stuff with him. I cried because I was excited and happy too. I cried for the whole fucking situation.

"How's our tiny little badass today sis?" Gin whisper shouts at my stomach, touching my belly as he sits down next to me at the bar. The cat is out of the bag, or should I say, the baby is sticking out from the belly. Everyone knows. Everyone's excited. A few days ago, I visited my dad and told him before it got back to him. I wanted him to hear it from me.

I'd never been a fan of jails, but I hate them even more now that my dad is locked away in one. I hate having to visit him through glass. I hated seeing him cuffed and shackled. Sitting down at the glass visiting window, I picked up the phone and waited for him to do the same. I watch and wait for him.

Clothed in an orange jump suit, he worked his way to me, followed by two guards. Passing people who were already seated at their visiting windows, they all give him a respectful chin lift, and he returned them. Once his eyes landed on me though, his face lit up like a fucking Christmas tree. Those tired eyes brightened for me. And for the first time in a long time, he smiled. He sat down and grabbed the phone instantly.

"Doll face," he greeted me softly. Just hearing his gruff voice and seeing his face made me teary eyed.

"Hi dad. I miss you." A sad smile touched his lips and he nodded once.

"I know baby."

"How are you dad?"

"Survivin'."

"You eating okay? You need anything. Are people treating you alright?"

He laughed and shook his head at me. I worry about him in there 'cause I'm not there to keep an eye on him to make sure he's eating well, or that he's got clean laundry. Hell, I worried about him when he was just sitting at the club.

"I'm okay Lilly. Foods shit, but I get commissary. People are people in here." He wouldn't tell me even if shit was bad, but he looked alright. Tired, but okay.

"I've got some news." He was excited for me. He was happy to be a grandpa.

"So imma Pops now, huh?" He said thoughtfully with a smile on his face. I told him all the baby details. I filled him in on all the good things happening and it seemed to make him happy. He looked like he enjoyed hearing about all things baby. No need to lay all the bad shit on him. Surprisingly, he didn't bring much up about Tank. He just told me to take care of myself and the baby.

"Love ya doll face."

I left him with that happy news. I knew he was happy for me, but there was regret there too. I know his decision to turn himself in weighs on him and I know it bothers him that he's not here with me to help, not here for his brothers, the club. And now he won't be here for the baby. But he lives with his decision, because he knows he was protecting his family. It's always bitter sweet to visit him.

Everyone else around the club seems excited about the baby too. Some of the guys could care less either way, but the majority of the guys seem happy about it. Of course all the ladies are excited for the baby. They're all baby whores and can't wait to get their hands on my baby. The ladies are excited to cuddle and kiss on my baby. Of course, all the guys say shit like they can't wait to put him on his first bike, take him to his first strip club, or give him his first sip of beer. For the record, none of that is happening until my baby is thirty. According to all the guys, I'm having a boy and none will hear that it may be a girl. Most of the Old Ladies want a girl. It's a tossup really. At times like this, I really wish my mom and dad were here to join in of the baby debate. They could enjoy their first, and probably only, grandbaby. If I think about it too much I'll cry, so I stuff it away with all my other feelings I can't and don't want to deal with.

"Baby's not hard of hearing Gin." Leo chuckles from a few stools down.

"Well *he's* in there floatin' 'round in water. You ever hear under water? Yeah, it's fuckin' impossible."

"Amniotic fluid." I correct him.

"Shut up. That is one gross fuckin' word." Tags mumbles as he walks by making a gagging noise.

Gin punches his shoulder as he walks by and says, "Placenta." Slow and drawn out.

Tag proceeds to gag and shake his head. "Fuckin' hate you, asshole."

"Doin' your baby homework?" I tease Gin on his baby words. He shrugs and smiles sheepishly. Peaches has been a little baby crazy since we found out. At first she was sick about it like me, but now that she has a new reason to shop and someone to dress up and spoil, she's okay with it. She's been cramming anything baby down Gin's throat, or anyone within ear shot. Stitch sits down next to Gin with a beer in his hand and just like they all do, he touches my belly. I thought it'd bother me, but it doesn't. It's their thing. They all do it so I let them have it. They consider my baby, our baby. We are family, so I totally get it.

"Somethin' like that." Gin says with an eye roll.

"You know it might be a girl." I tell them. Stitch chokes on his beer and glares at me right along with Gin, who looks like he might throw up. Fuck, what's the issue?

"You don't want it to be a little girl?" I ask them. Stupid question, but it is fun to fuck with them. They both almost look squeamish when I say the word girl.

"It's a boy," Gin says with steel determination. He's pretty fucking sure of himself.

"No! No fuckin' girls. You have a girl, we might go crazy tryin' to keep the dicks away from her when she's sixteen if she looks like you did in high school."

"Yeah, we'll see. You two seen Tank around then?" Of course they all shake their heads. Everyone still seems to avoid all topics that have anything to do with Tank or I.

"Fine. I'll find him myself." I don't bother pushing for more, that's all I'm getting.

****

Pulling my Jeep into Tanks driveway, I feel a little unsure and nervous all of a sudden. Fifteen minutes ago when I left the club, I was brave and sure of myself. I was going to leave my feelings and emotions at the door and go in there and talk to him like an adult. Now I feel a little queasy. I'd decided I should tell him about my next appointment with the doctor. He wants to be included and he's trying, so I thought it'd be nice to have him there. Sitting in his driveway, I let the shitty worry work its way back up. What if he doesn't want to go? What if he's not interested? If he says no, I might cry and then kill him. I don't think I could handle that right now, so I stuff down my fear and remind myself that this is for my baby, and my feelings don't matter.

Walking up to the front door, I knock on the frame. It's strange to knock. I used to just walk right in and kick my shoes off and throw my purse on the couch. It feels wrong to knock when this used to be my house too. The front door's open, but the screen door's closed, so I knock again, but get nothing. Faintly I can hear some banging and a drill?

"Tank?" Still I get nothing. I came all this way and worked up my nerve so I'm not leaving now. Sticking my head inside I yell for him.

"Tank?" Taking a few steps inside, a pang of sadness hits my stomach. I feel fucking homesick. A deep sense of nostalgia tugs on my heart 'cause I miss this house. I miss being here. The living room looks exactly the same, and a single tear hits my cheek when I see my boots still sitting by the side door. He hasn't gotten rid of anything. It's all exactly the same. God, it's like it's all waiting for me. Being in here makes me long for when I lived here, when this was my house too.

Walking down the hall I call for him again. "Tank?"

"Yeah babe. Back here."

His deep gruff voice makes me smile. It's a sad smile, but a smile nonetheless. I follow the banging and his voice down the hall to the spare room. Looking inside, I find Tank crouched down and he's putting together a … crib? A fucking crib. Jesus Christ, it's a crib. It's big and black and fucking perfect. Instantly the tears start. Fucking pregnancy hormones are turning me into a sad ass mess. Goddamn crib.

"Hey babe, you alright?" He jumps right up and makes his way to me, concern worn all over his handsome face.

"What's wrong Lil?" his hands are on my sides pulling me closer. Shaking my head I wipe those goddamn tears away and step back. I can't be this close to him when he's building my baby a crib. Why does he have to be so goddamn sweet when I still want to hate him?

"I'm fine," I sniffle like a loser.

Touching my stomach softly, he looks into my eyes. "You sure?"

"Yeah. I'm good." I lie. I lie like an asshole. I'm not good, I'm a mess of pathetic pregnant hormones.

"What the fuck's the tears about?"

"That *thing*." I wave my hand toward that thing, that goddamn crib. I can't look at it and I don't want to talk about it. Stupid crib is making me cry. Stupid hormones and stupid crib.

"The crib. Is it wrong? Shit! Baby if it's not right, I'll buy whatever fuckin' crib you want." He looks heartbroken suddenly and completely unsure and now I feel like a bitch. These motherfucking hormones are going to kill me. God and he's being so fucking sweet. Damn it all to hell.

"No, the crib is fine."

"Then why the fuck you cryin' at me? What's goin' on baby?"

I can't look at his face. I can't look at him looking at me with love, concern and care. I can't be in *his* house looking at that *crib* while *he* builds it for *our* baby. I can't do this.

"I've got a doctor's appointment in two weeks. You can come if you want to." I barely choke out. I turn and walk out before I do something I'll regret, like start crying, or climbing him like a tree.

I can't do this shit anymore. I want to give up and give in so fucking bad.

15
Crazy

Tank

Sitting at the bar with Stitch, we're talking about adding some new brothers when a loud, "Fuck!", followed by a crash that has us both out of our seats, on our feet, and in that office so goddamn fast I'm surprised Stitch didn't spill his beer.

"What the fuck you doin'?" Ripping through the door, I almost trip over a tipped over box. There are papers everywhere, a bottle of bleach and some paper towels. Lil's sitting on the office floor in a mess. A serious annoyed pout on those plump lips and the death scowl on that face.

"Nothing'." She snaps up at me.

"Don't look like nothing'. You need a hand?"

"Not from you." She grumbles. Thought we were getting past the hate? Apparently not, because she's throwing it out at me with her eyes.

"You got an issue with me?" Stupid question really. Hell yeah, she's got an issue with me. She always does.

"*Issues?* Yeah Tank I've got issues with you." Throwing a hand out, I allow princess to go on with her attitude.

"Care to elaborate." Standing up, she grumbles at me.

"*Your* baby is killin' my back. I can't lift shit anymore. And I'm tryin' to clean this nasty, dirty whore infested office." With a stomp, she slams past me, shoves her elbow into my side, and walks out the door. *My* baby? Stitch looks at me and back at the door Lil's feisty ass just stomped through.

"Pregnancy makes her bitchy." Stitch points out with wide scared eyes.

Fuck yeah, it does.

This is how my life has been, full of an emotional ass woman. Lil doesn't give me much time, and the time I get is usually full of crazy. It's like she saves that shit up just for me. I'm talking crazy. Not her usual crazy, this is a whole new special brand. Nine times outta ten she's yelling at me, blaming me for something, or calling the baby *mine.* My guess is when the baby is doing something she doesn't like, it belongs to me.

I'm not gonna lie, I still fucking like it when she says *your baby.* At least she's acknowledging me. At the very least, she's including me. As pathetic as that makes me, I just don't fucking care. As long as she's including me somehow, I'll take it.

And every once in a while I get tears from her. Those usually come after she's yelled at me and then she says it's my 'sad eyes' that make her feel guilty, and then she cries. No fucking clue what 'sad eyes' are, but I guess I have them and they make her fucking crazy. If she was any other bitch, this shit wouldn't fly, but for me, some attitude is sure the fuck better than nothing at all from her, but don't let those tears fool you. They last five seconds before she's right back to screaming at me, throwing and breaking shit, and giving attitude to every person within ear shot. Mean Lil is now my reality, but fuck it, I'll take it.

****

"The Jeeps makin' this *'clink, clunk, tink'* noise." Lil says, shoving her keys at me. I try hard not to laugh, but it's not easy.

"Could you make that noise again babe?"

Slapping my chest hard she says, "You're an asshole."

"Gotcha'. You've told me enough, I know."

"So … can you look at it for me?" She barks at me, arms crossed under those big tits of hers. Does she really think she needs to ask me that shit? My ass has never been able to tell her no. Fixing her Jeep is no exception.

Oh, now she's getting extra annoyed as she shifts, putting her hand on her hip, and starts to tap her foot impatiently. Today she seems to be filled with a little extra fire.

"I don't know. Can I?" Yep. Extra fire. Spinning around with her hair flyin', she glares. Narrowing those brown eyes, she kills me with those babies. Probably shouldn't poke the angry mama bear, but I just can't help myself. Fuck I miss her. I miss her so much I'll take her crazy like a starving fucking man.

"Don't fuck with me today, *Roman*." Yeah she's in a fucking mood. Fuck, what I wouldn't give just to bend her ass over the tool bench and drive home. Balls smacking against her ass, hands in hair. Fuck …

"Broke out the name I see, baby."

"I'm not your baby." She spits, giving her eyes a good roll. Like me calling her that is fucking absurd. How fucking wrong she is.

"The fuck you aren't. Six feet under … Nah, not even then. You're mine Lil, forever and always. Get fuckin' used to it."

"Fuck! You're impossible."

"Yeah, well at least I'm not fuckin' crazy, baby."

Her retreating back, finger in the air, and a "Fuck you!" Is what I'm left with. I've got to be as fucking crazy, if not more than her, because that shit just makes me smile. I love that fire. I love it so goddamn much.

****

Dodging the pelting rain, I head into Gin's without a knock. He called me over here in a hurry. He's not getting a fucking courtesy knock.

"What the fuck took you so long?"

"Puttin' one of those dresser changing things together. Stupid piece of shit."

"Not workin' out for you, Handy Tank?"

"Shut the fuck up. You know that shit is so goddamn cheap. Not havin' my baby in that shit. I'll just build one."

"Come on man, the mess is in the garage."

We pushed around a shit ton of boxes, all full of Peaches shit. That bitch is a fucking pack rat. No doubt that garage will be filled right the fuck back up in a few weeks.

"I need a beer or something."

Walking into the kitchen, that hardened piece of meat in my chest stutters. I can feel her. That shit is physical. Lil's sitting on the kitchen counter, feet swinging, smile on her beautiful fucking face. I can see my baby today. She's wearing a tight white shirt with her arms folded over that tiny stomach, just resting there. I have to remind myself to keep my hands to myself. I have to remind myself to keep to myself. Fuck it.

Taking two steps into the kitchen, she notices me. Her big browns snap up to me and there's no glare, no eye roll this time. I can't stop myself. That's all the invitation I need. Today she doesn't completely fucking hate me. I don't know why I fucking do it, I'm sure it's probably sheer stupidity, or it could be the lack of blood in my brain that had relocated to my dick from just seeing her. Might be the desperation. I just can't keep my hands to myself. I need to touch her. I need that shit like oxygen.

Pushing between those thick thighs, I go for a cup I have no goddamn use for, just to get close to her, to feel her. She doesn't push me away, but she doesn't touch me either. I can smell her. She smells sugary and sweet, just like I remember. I want more. Fuck I need it so bad I can feel it. Wrapping that long soft hair around my hand I bury my face in her neck. Skin on a little bit of skin. That small stomach pressed into mine, I hold her to me. This is as much as I've gotten in months. Fuck, I've needed this. Shit feels like home, where I should be.

Then I hear it. A soft, quiet sob as her body shakes lightly against mine. I pushed too far. I wished I felt bad about it, but I don't. I just don't fucking care. I needed that shit.

"Please don't," she chokes out. That's all I'm getting. Stepping back from her, I see those dark eyes, tear filled and broken.

"Why?" Her voice is soft and strangled.

"Fuck Lil, I'm not sorry." It's all I can say, because I'm not fuckin' sorry. I'll never be sorry for wanting to touch her. No goddamn way in hell I'll ever be sorry for loving my woman.

Pushing me away, she fixes the tears and gives me a lip curling glare. There's that hate.

Hopping off the counter, my stomach dips watching her do that shit. Fuck. I wish she wouldn't do that. She could fall or some shit. She's trying to give me a heart attack.

"Be careful Lil. Damn." And just like that, it's over. She's no longer heartbroken, she's back to being mad at me. I opened my mouth and sweet sad Lil has left the motherfucking building.

"Don't tell me shit."

"Baby, just worried about you hurting yourself."

"No you're not. You're only worried about me hurtin' the baby." She can't believe that shit. She knows I love her. Fuck, if anything happened to either of them it'd fucking kill me.

"That's bullshit n' you know it."

"Do I?" She throws back at me. Those eyes are masked with mean, but there's that heartbreak in there too. It might be buried deep, but it's there. She's pretty fuckin' good at hiding that shit from me, but I've become better at seeing the hurt through all that other shit. She might fool everyone around us, but not for one single fucking second does she fool me. I know she's hurt.

"Lil, you know I fuckin' love you. I'll love you 'till the day I fuckin' die. Don't ever doubt that shit. You might hate me right now n' I fuckin' get it, but that shit doesn't change how much I love your ass."

16

Car Seats

&

Kitchen Counters

Lil

I try to hold onto that hate. I feed off that mean woman I've become so I can use it. I have to. If I let it go, I'll break and give in. If I let it go, I'll run straight for Tank and forget everything. I would push it all away just to have him back and part of me is scared shitless over it.

But part of me says let it go. Forgive him and move on. No use in dwelling, right? What I wouldn't give to have all that back, having Tank to myself again. I'd love to be able to wrap myself around him, to touch him, kiss him, and to love him without worry and fear. I want him back.

As much as I want to, I just can't fucking forget. Another part of me says this is just temporary. He's pulling it together enough to get me back, then he'll get comfortable, and things will fall to shit again. He'll get me back around and he'll start remembering, and then push me away. I'll start to lose the Tank I'm seeing now and I can't go through that again, and I don't want to see him go through it again either. I don't think I'll survive it. And I will not put my child through that. I'm not ready to fight that fight just yet.

So I hold onto the hate and anger. I hold onto the mean. It's not like I set out to be mean to him every time I see him. I don't want to push him away from me, but I can't help it. He smiles at me. He touches me. He's soft with me and all that bad shit filters back in. Was this how he was feeling with me? I wouldn't know 'cause he never said anything. I just don't wanna go through that again. So I protect my heart, along with my baby's heart. I wait it out until my heart's ready. I wait until I feel it. I wait until I know I can trust him again.

"What the hell are you doin'?" Tanks gruff face pops out of the back seat of my Jeep when I kick through the front door of the club. He just stares at me like I'm speaking French.

"You and Gin, what the fuck are you doin'?" I ask, pointing at the two of them for clarification, in case me staring right at him didn't give him the hint. Still he stares. Tools, an empty box, and my back seat sitting on the cement of the clubs front lot. He just ignores me. Gin just ignores me. What the fuck?

Tugging on the back door, I look inside and around Tanks giant body.

"What the hell? Why'd you take the seat out?"

"Had to anchor this fuckin' pain in the ass in."

"What?" I'm so goddamn confused. Shoving a gray car seat base at me he grumbles.

"This stupid fuckin' thing has to be anchored to your goddamn car. Had to take the seat out." He's putting in the car seat? My heart hurts, squeezing in my chest. Suddenly I'm not quite as mad at him as I was ten seconds ago. Why is he taking care of this? I feel tears well up in my eyes.

I can't stand here while he's being sweet. "Whatever. Just make sure to put my back seat back in."

Locking myself in the bathroom, I let the tears come. I cry like a baby. Damn it. Why? He's making this so fucking hard. His big body crammed into the back of my Jeep, looking uncomfortable and mad. Too big to be in the back of my Jeep, yet there he was, doing it for my baby. A knock on the door startles me.

"What?" I snap at the door.

"Baby, what's wrong?"

"Go away Tank!"

And he does. He leaves. My car is fixed when I let myself out the bathroom. The seat's back to its original spot with a car seat securely set in my back seat. It's facing the right way too, mirror attached to my mirror so I can see the baby. Jesus Christ, there's even a toy hanging on the handle of the car seat. Damn him.

****

Five bags. I can do this. Loading up my arms, I make the trek up to my back door. My back hurts and I do not feel like making extra trips in and out. I just want to unload my groceries, find my sweats, and plop down on my couch. Pushing through my front door, I see a pair of dirty CATS propped up on my coffee table. Seriously? Bright mean blue eyes find me.

"What the fuck Lil?" Hopping up, Tank runs over to me. "Why the fuck are you carryin' all this shit in at once?"

"Why are you here? Better yet, how'd you get in?" Picking up my bags, he looks up at me like I'm crazy for asking. I guess it is a stupid question.

"How the fuck you think I got in?" He shoots back at me.

"Stop pickin' my goddamn locks. One of my neighbors will see you, they're gonna call the cops, *Roman*." Sitting my bags on the kitchen counter, he glares at me.

"Call me Roman again, imma smack the shit outta you." He's so full of shit, his eyes should be brown.

"What do you want, *Roman*?"

"Fuck," he mutters under his breath, shaking his head. It's a little fun to pick back at him. I know he hates when I call him Roman and sometimes I just can't help it.

"So why'd you pick my locks? Lookin' for a B and E charge?"

Hopping up onto the counter, he starts digging through my bags, looking for ... who the fuck knows what. So casual. So at home. It's so normal it starts to hurt. This is the shit I miss the most. The normal every day shit I don't get because he fucked it all up.

"Like your dress babe." He nods at my strapless maxi dress. He only likes it because it's easy access to my tits.

"Don't avoid my question *Roman*." Grabbing a handful of grapes, he pops one into his sexy mouth. He stands and stares at me as he chews. Today he looks extra scruffy. He really needs a good shave. His gray tee is dirty and greasy, same with the jeans, but he looks good. So good. Too good.

"Just wanted to come check on you babe." He's a liar.

Those crystal blue eyes are dark and mean while he watches me, that face rough and sexy. It reminds me of the first time I saw him, all that big, mean man. I miss touching him so much that I dream about it most nights. Waking up, hot and needy. I want him.

"Fuck me."

Turning his head slowly back toward me, he looks at me like I've lost my mind.

"Please?" I go with it. I shut my mind down before I can talk myself out of how fucking stupid I am. I shouldn't want him. I shouldn't want this, but I do. I want it so bad I can't take it.

"You really just say that? Or did I imagine that shit?"

"Don't make me say it again." I plead.

"No. I want to hear you say it again Lil." He demands.

"You heard me."

He's off the counter and on me in a second with his hands around my body, pulling me to him. Wrapping his big rough hands around my legs, he picks me up and my ass is set onto the counter. No amount of fight could stop him now. I opened my mouth and said the words. Do I feel wrong about it? Yes. But do I want his hands on me? Yes.

With his hand on the back of my neck, he pulls me in and his lips find mine. They're harsh and rough.

"You're right, I heard you." He says roughly around my lips. "You want it baby. Who am I to deprive you?" Running the tip of his tongue over the curve of my lower lip, he hums in admiration. I let it all go. For just these few moments, I pretend I'm not broken.

His rough, calloused fingers draw a path up my leg, slowly touching my skin. No panties, and he's working his way up. My skin tingles and burns, as my thighs clench in anticipation.

"What are you doing?" I damn well know what he's doing. I gave him the words and he's doing it. But then all that bad is trying to break free and fuck this up for me and the doubt settles in. His fingers stop on the inside of my thigh as he stops to look down at me, watching me.

"Do you want me to stop?" he asks. His voice hoarse and deep, and his beard is rubbing on my neck and shoulder. I can't talk.

Taking my silence as his cue, his fingers start again. At his harsh touch, I shut my mind down and go with it. God I've missed this. His other hand explores my naked back, siding a single finger up and down my spine. My body arches into his. I'm wet and ready, and those fingers are killing me slowly. I need him now.

Grabbing his shirt, I tug him as close as I can get him. My legs are wrapped around his hips as I press myself into him. I can't get close enough. Looking into his eyes, I ask for it again.

"Fuck me."

"Baby, yeah. I got you." Two long skilled fingers push into me. "I've always got you." Filling me, stretching me. So goddamn good. Letting my head drop onto his shoulder I just feel him. Letting my body feel him, focusing on the sensations. He has one hand on my thigh, fingers digging into my skin that are holding my legs open wide for him. The other hand works me over. His fingers are fucking me into a mess. This isn't like the last few times he's touched me. His touch isn't mean or mad. His touch is reverent this time. He's still rough like always, but there is no anger there.

Standing in between my legs I can feel how hard he is. I know he wants me. He's always so rough and hard, exactly how I like him. I should be pissed at myself for giving into him, but the truth is, I love him. How can I not?

His fingers are so skilled with my body, making me hot, making that fire burn. Ripping off his shirt, I pull him as close as I can get him. His mouth is on my skin, teeth biting my shoulder and neck. Those hard blue eyes come to my face and fixate on me, taking everything in. His own private show while his fingers work into me, dragging them slowly back out, watching me.

"Right … *there*." So close.

"Right there?" he growls. Slowing his movements, he's teasing me. I need more. Grabbing his wrist, I try to urge him on, but he pulls back.

He stops all together. My legs still around him, he pulls his fingers out, and gone is my impending orgasm. With a devilish smile, he licks his fingers clean, slowly dragging each one over his tongue, sucking me off his fingers slowly. His eyes are burning with trouble.

"You're filthy," I tell him honestly.

"And you fuckin' love it." He states firmly. I do, but I hate that I do.

Letting my hands trail up his arms to the back of his neck, I wind my hands into his hair. It's been so long since I've touched him like this. Tugging his head down to me, I lick a path up his neck to his ear, biting and sucking my way up his soft skin. Both of his hands rest on my thighs, leaning into me. I make my way up and I bite down on his earlobe. He tries to pull away from me, but I lock my legs around him. He's not leaving now.

"Give it to me motherfucker."

I've never wanted anything more than I want this right fucking now, and he knows it too. He's going to hold this against me tomorrow 'cause tonight, I gave him the upper hand. I need the connection again just for this small amount of time. I need to feel something. With a dirty smirk on his lips, he pushes my dress up over my hips. He's enjoying himself. This is his game now.

"Please, Tank." I beg with tears in my eyes. I can't hold it in.

No need to ask him twice. He takes only a second to release himself and begins slamming into me. I feel that shit everywhere and I bite down on his shoulder to keep my scream in. I am full and sated, and I finally feel whole again. Body on body. It's not right that I asked this of him, but I had to. I needed it so goddamn bad. I needed him.

17

Fat Girl Pants

Tank

Everyday gets a little better. Everyday gets a little easier.

Last night she let me back in. I got an hour of that shit. I got an

hour of what I used to have with her. It wasn't just sex, it wasn't

just fucking her on a kitchen counter. For the first time in a long

fucking time, she needed me. She wanted me. That gave me

hope. Then as soon as she let me in, she shut me out. But I was in

for that few moments and that shit, in my opinion, is progress. I

just need to wear her down. Fuck it, I will wear her down if it's the

last motherfucking thing I do.

I get to see her most days. I get to see her and my baby

and that makes all this shit a little bit easier on me. I get that time

I so fucking desperately need. She's letting me come to a doctor's appointment, she's not ignoring me, and sometimes I can get that smile that melts all the mean in me. That's something to look forward to. That is something to be fucking thankful for. She's letting me back in. Slowly but surely, we'll get there. We fucking have to 'cause I won't live without her or our baby. That shit isn't even an option for me.

****

Pulling into my driveway, it's raining hard. So damn hard I had to take my truck to the club. Pulling up to my garage, my headlights shine on my front porch. What the fuck?

Throwing the truck in park, I hop out into the rain like a fuckin' lunatic. My stomach drops to my feet and I almost break my goddamn neck trying to get out of my truck and to her before she disappears, like a mirage.

"What the fucks wrong Lil?" She's sitting on my porch, her back leaning against my door and her knees pulled up to her chest. She offers me a weak smile as I make my way toward her. All kinds of crazy shit starts flying around in my head.

"You alright?" Standing over her she looks up at me with those dark, heart breaking eyes.

"I miss you."

****

Lil's sitting on the couch in my tee. Her hair's a mess, curls everywhere. She's got a pair of my gray wool, heavy duty work socks on her feet, the ones with the red band around the top. Damn things go to her knees. This is something I never thought I'd ever fucking see again. Shit makes me so goddamn happy my chest is bursting with it.

"You need anything baby?" I ask her. Shoving the spoon full of ice cream into her mouth, she smiles around the spoon and shakes her head. I've missed this and if she tries leaving, I'm fucking tying her ass up.

"I give up Tank." She tells me quietly. Again my heart stops. Those words could go either way.

"Give up what babe?" I ask her as calmly as possible. I try not to sound like the miserable prick I've become. I try not to scare her with my fucking desperation. Scooping a giant spoonful of ice cream up, she crams it into her mouth and shrugs one shoulder.

"Fightin' it."

"Lil, I ain't followin' you. Just say what you mean, without a mouthful of ice cream."

In fact, she's fuckin' scaring me. If she moves that ass from my couch, I'm not above holding her here against her will. I'll barricade the fuck outta my front door to keep her here.

"I'm done fightin' you. I don't have it in me anymore. I'm more miserable than I was before I left. I just can't do this shit anymore. I just hope you'll keep getting better and you'll start letting me back in. I've never wanted you to hurt, and I'm so sorry that I caused you the pain of watching that shit happen to me."

I fall to my knees in front of her, looking at this beautiful woman who I tore down so relentlessly. How could I have done all this to her?

"I'm done babe. Not gonna put that shit on you anymore. I've been working so hard on getting myself through it, and don't ever apologize to me for what happened to you. I'm sorry for letting all my insecurities get dumped onto you. I should have talked to you, or anybody about it, I just didn't see anyone fixin' it for me. But I'm fixin' it Lil. I swear to you, I'm here for you, and we will work through any shit that comes at us."

She doesn't say anything. I wait for something, anything.

"I still love you." She tells me a moment later. I feel a weight lifted. I feel like I can fucking breath again 'cause those are the words I needed to hear. Fuck I needed them.

"I know you do." Cocking that beautiful head to the side, she raises that damn eyebrow. "You think so?"

"Yeah, I fuckin' do." I know she loves me because if she didn't, then none of this shit would have bothered her. She's strong as fuck and the shit I threw at her wouldn't have mattered if she didn't fucking love me. She would have walked away a long time ago. My baby wouldn't have cried over someone she didn't love, and I wouldn't have been able to break her heart. I know she loves me because she wouldn't have fought for me, for us, if she didn't. It's all right there in those big, brown, heart breaking eyes.

"Cocky fuckin' asshole," she scoffs and rolls her eyes at me.

"Goddamn right. Never gonna change, babe."

****

We watch TV in silence. We started off at opposite ends of the couch, but I let that shit go for about five minutes before I drug her across the couch to me. I can't sit here next to her. That shit doesn't work for me. I needed to fucking touch her and if it meant dragging her across the couch, then that's exactly what I was doing. She didn't fight me, which is good because I was not in the mood to get into it with her. I just want to lie here and hold her. Feel her, be close to her.

Throwing her arms above her head, she stretches and turns into me with her face pressed into my chest and one of her legs go between mine, and that tiny ass bump is pressed into my stomach.

"That thing get in the way?" I ask her. Out of nowhere, she starts laughing. She laughs so hard she can barely fucking breathe. I love that sound. I let her laugh and enjoy it while I get it too.

"Yes and no. I can't sleep on my stomach anymore. Pants are starting to become an issue."

"You need new pants babe?"

"Yes. Big, fat girl pants." She grumbles into my chest. Even if she was nine months pregnant, I doubt she'd need *fat girl* pants, whatever the fuck fat girl pants are.

"Doubt that baby. You'd be hot as fuck, even if you get huge."

"I wanna hear you say that in nine months when I look like I ate a couple brothers."

She wants to hear me say it in nine months? Even if she doesn't realize it, those few words give me enough hope to cling to. I'm that fucking desperate for her. I latch onto any and every word of hope she'll feed me. Meaning to or not, she fed me all the hope I need.

"I should go," Lil says a while later. It's late and storming pretty bad. We've been lying on this couch for hours and I'll be damned if she thinks she's goin' somewhere.

"You're stayin' babe." I tell her.

Lifting her head up off my chest, she cocks her head slowly. I know I'm about to get a fight. Any other time I would have been down. We could fight, then make up, and fuck. Now, I'm scared as hell that anything I say might have her running away from me.

Scooting up and off of the couch, she stands up and I know she's about to head for the front door, and that needy panic starts to wash over me. Turning on her heels, she heads for the hall instead. My heart stutters to a fucking stop. Looking over her shoulder at me, she smiles.

"You comin' baby?"

****

Standing by the bathroom door I watch her crawl into my bed. Our bed. Throwing the blankets over her head she wiggles down under all the sheets and blankets, getting comfortable. In times like this, I have to believe there's someone out there on my side. Someone's looking down at me and throwing good shit my way. I have needed this for so long. I missed her so much that part of me wonders if this is too good to be true. I'm scared to death that any minute she might be gone and I'll be stuck feeling like I'm dying all over again. I'm pretty fuckin' sure me feeling this way is unhealthy. It's probably not a good idea to be so dependent of another person for your own happiness, but here she is making me feel like I'm finally able to live and breathe again. I'm finally able to be happy again.

Poking her head back up and out of the blankets, she smiles a soft, sad smile at me.

"This is all I ever wanted." She says quietly with a touch of apprehension. I couldn't agree more.

"You here for good Lil?" I can't let it rest. I need to know that she's here permanently. I know I'm jumping the goddamn gun here and she might feel pressured, but there is no other way for me. This is how I do shit. There is no waiting for me. She was mine before and she has to be mine again. I can't live any other way.

She nods slowly and thoughtfully.

"Yes. But we still have shit to talk about and things that need worked out."

And I've no doubt that we do. That girl is not going to let me back in that easily. Just like everything else, she's gonna make me work for it. And I will. I'll work every second of every goddamn day for the rest of my life for it. I'll work for that girl 'til I have nothing left, or 'till I'm dead and buried. I'll do whatever I have to.

"You gonna stand there all night and stare at me, or are you gonna get in here and cuddle with me and your baby?" Cuddle with her and my baby. Never thought I'd hear those words. But then again, I never thought I'd have Lil in my life. Never thought I could love someone so much.

"Education Lil, I don't cuddle." I tell her seriously. She snorts a laugh and rolls her eyes at me. She doesn't believe a word I'm saying, with good reason.

"Okay you fuckin' bad ass. Get in here and feel me up then."

****

The club door kicks open. Lil walks that fine ass in wearing some cut off jean shorts and a tight ass tee. I can see that hot little bump under her shirt; our baby. I love the fuck out of that shit. We came in this morning together. She's stayed with me since she came over those few nights ago and I couldn't be any fuckin' happier about it either. She left a while ago with Peaches to do whatever girls do. I'm still a little fucking twitchy about being apart from her; A lingering fear that she won't come back, but I do my best to ignore it … At least I try to.

Walking in, she's holding a shit ton of bags and boxes. Walking right up to me, she dumps that shit on my lap before I get the chance to stand up. I hate watching her carry that kind of shit. Isn't that shit bad for her and the baby?

"What the fuck is all this shit?" I get a sweet smile and trouble in those eyes. Turning on her heels, she marches that ass right back out the door without an answer. Alright …

Picking up a bag, I open it up to find baby shit of every variety.

"Well that's scary as fuck." Rampage says looking a tad sick. It might be if I didn't love Lil so much. I just shrug and push some of the shit off me and onto Gin. Lil comes back in and sets a few more things on the couch by Gin and me. Sticking his hand inside the bag, Gin pulls out the worlds smallest baby outfit.

"He gonna be that fuckin' small?" Gin asks looking up at Lil with the weirdest fuckin' expression on his face.

She shrugs and says, "Sure as hell don't feel like it since I feel huge already, but babies are usually born between six and eight pounds. Sometimes more, sometimes less."

Damn. I didn't realize they were that small. So maybe this is scarier than I thought. I like that we're all calling the baby a 'he'. I keep telling Lil I don't think I can handle a girl. I'll love either one, but the idea of a little tiny Lil scares the fuck out of me on so many levels.

****

Lil's in my bed again tonight. We haven't had that "talk" yet, but I have a feeling it's coming. She's naked in my bed and that's all that fucking matters. Looking at her, it all kinda makes sense. It's all about her. The quicker I would have realized that shit, the better off I would've been. Something I've been learning since meeting Lil is men don't run shit. We're gonna talk when she wants to. Yeah, I'm about to get kicked the fuck out the man club, they're gonna take my balls for this shit, but it's the motherfuckin' truth. They run us. Women give birth to us. Women raise us. It's a woman you fuck, you marry, you have kids with. She's not gonna do shit unless she wants to, and any man who forces that shit on her is not a man. Yeah women, they run this motherfucker. I've learned real quick it's not me in charge anymore.

I run my club. I've killed. I've done my time. I've fucked up plenty of lives, but Lil owns *my* life, and she'll do whatever the fuck she wants with it and like a fucking sucker, I'll let her because I love her. Fuck, I'm not sure I'd have it any other way really. She's on the back of *my* bike, in *my* house, in *my* bed, on *my* dick, then she can do whatever the fuck she wants because it's with me. She wants to lead me around by my balls, fine. Lead away baby, and I know that Lil will always love and take care of me. I absolutely see this now and only wish that I did it sooner.

You want to keep your bitch happy you'll learn real quick she's in charge.

"Tank?" She whispers, her head on my chest. I've been waiting for this. It's three in the morning and I can't sleep. For the first time in a long fucking time, it has nothing to do with that night or those scars. Tonight I'm up because I still can't believe she's here. I still can't believe that my baby is mine again and shit's finally coming back around.

"Baby, yeah?" Setting her chin in my chest, she looks at me. "Did you fuck Trix?" Didn't expect that to come off of those lips right off of the bat.

"Lil…" With this shit, I'll proceed with caution.

"I don't care if you did. Well, I care, but I think I can get over it." Her words are sad. She shouldn't get over it.

"Baby. That ain't shit you just forget about." I know I fucked up and I'm not cruel enough not to admit it. She deserves the truth.

"I won't forget, but I'll work to get over it. I don't want the baby to not have you."

Fuck. As much as it hurts to say it, I tell her, "Lil, don't stay with me just for the baby. I'll be here for that baby one way or another. Don't get me wrong, I want you. I'll always want you.

You're it for me, but I don't want you here of you feel stuck."

Those words were some of the hardest I've ever said. Pretty much

gave her an out. As much as I hate it, if she wants out, I gotta let

her go. I love her enough to let her go if that's what she needs

from me.

"Did you fuck her?" She asks me again with steel reserve in

that sweet voice. Silently I shrug, because I don't fucking know. I

couldn't remember that night to save my life. I saw that key and

that was it. If I could go back and change anything besides that

night I almost lost Lil, that'd be it.

"Don't fuckin' know?"

"If you did, did it mean anything to you?" That's' easy.

"Fuck no. Come on Lil, you're the only woman I've ever

wanted. Only woman I'd ever be callin' my Old Lady."

"Okay then. I can get over it. I want you, and I want to

know you still want me."

"Education Lil. I'll always fuckin' want you. You're it for me woman."

She nods once and seems satisfied. Kissing my chest she says, "Okay Tank." But she's not done, she hits me with another one.

"Did you kiss her?" She growls this time. With that question there's pain in her eyes. That question was harder for her to ask, because I can tell she really doesn't want to know. I don't kiss those bitches though. I have no clue what and where their mouths have been.

"Babe you know I don't kiss gash." For some sick reason, she's relieved I didn't kiss her. I could be blacked out drunk and I wouldn't kiss the whores. This is something that's fact around the club. Not once over the years, no matter how fucked up and blacked out I've been, that was always a concern for the whores, why I never once kissed any of them.

"Then I can get over you possibly fuckin' her. Kissing is so much more personal." If she says so. Kissing my chest again she adds, "I just want you back in my life. I want to be where you are."

18
Time

Lil

Four months later ...

It's almost been a year since that night. These past nine months have been some of the hardest I've ever endured. I felt like I was fighting an unwinnable battle most of that time. It's been a constant uphill battle, but finally I can see the light at the end of the tunnel; the silver lining. Things are still gonna be rough and hard as hell, but Tank and I will have to fight for *us*. We are never gonna be perfect, or without our problems, but then again, when is life ever easy? We both have to want it enough to fight for it, and with all my heart, I know we will.

The Tank I knew before that night would have fought for me or he would've died trying. Slowly but surely, that Tank's has begun to come back to me, along with that fight. He's still gruff, rough, bossy, and he's still most definitely a rude fucking asshole.

But he loves me to death. He's letting me in and he's keeping me close. I have to believe that he'll keep getting better, and I finally have enough trust that things will keep getting better for us. If not, then I need to move on. We all make mistakes and fuck up. That's exactly what Tank did, and because I love him, I have to be willing to put that behind us and move forward for my baby, him, and myself. I want my family back and I'll fight for all three of us if I have to.

＊＊＊＊

My legs are slung low around his waist, knees bent up and my thighs are spread wide. His rock solid hips move with every lazy stroke of his cock as he grinds into me. His fingers are entwined with mine on each side of my head as he moves in and out of me slowly. This is something he never does, slow and easy, but right now I can't get enough of this feeling. This is the most intimate we've ever been and I can't help but love this slow burn building up in me with his slow and delicious movements. This is a whole new sensation for me.

He watches me with every move he makes as I bite my lip to the point of pain. He's wearing that grin I love to hate, and I know he's enjoying this. The only things that are touching are our hands and legs, which is making the urge to grab his hair harder to resist. That slow burn is building even more and I need what I know he can give me.

"I need more, Tank. I need what you love to give me."

His control must be shit now. He raises himself up and slowly pulls out of me, only to slam back into me with such force that I slide further up the bed. He holds himself balls deep in me and just stares at me like I'm the only woman in this world for him. I give him a smile.

He pulls out slowly, just to slam back in, but now he's with me. He begins to quicken his pace as he watches his cock slam into me, over and over. He lifts my legs only to spread them wider and forces himself deeper.

"Fuck, I want more Tank."

"Whatever you want baby."

He started this so slow and lazy, but now his arms and neck are straining and his breath is getting rougher. He gives it to me and he does it with the force I need and want. I love watching his body move when he fucks me, especially when I know he's so close to coming. He keeps up the pace and we're both sweating and slamming together so hard that I can't hold my orgasm. I scream with the force of it, especially while he continues his amazing assault. I feel myself tightening around him as he finally finds his own release and keeps up his pace till he's completely spent.

As my euphoria begins to wear off, he begins that slow and lazy move again, and just by looking at him, I know he's not even close to being finished. I'll do this slow and lazy, fast and hard dance with him all night long.

"Fuck, I love you baby." He says with the biggest smile on his face.

"I love you too, but whatever you do, just don't stop.

****

"Fuckin' gross sis," Stitch mumbles and looks like he might gag.

"Shut the fuck up man. She's feedin' my baby." Tank says and smacks the back of Stitches head when he walks into the room.

"Damn motherfucker, she stuffed down that entire big ass jar of pickles. Pretty sure that shit ain't healthy."

"Shut it!" I tell him around a mouth full of deliciousness. The baby and me want pickles for lunch, so we're eating pickles for lunch. I'm sitting on the couch with my jar of pickles propped on my rounded belly and a chocolate shake in my hand. I've fallen victim to the disturbing pregnancy cravings. I held out for a while, but there was absolutely no fighting them. They took over. I haven't wanted anything like chalk or dirt, but I'm really into the salty and sweet things. I eat pretty much anything and Tank gets us whatever we want.

Setting my jar down, I waddle my chunky ass to the baby's room.

"C'mere babe." Tank follows behind me, stomping and dragging his damn feet like a big ass baby.

"Every time I come in here, we end up at some fuckin' store, neck deep in baby shit babe."

"Tank." Is all I have to say. He groans and follows me anyway.

I moved back in here three months ago. Not so much as moved, but had my shit put back in the house for me. I got two weeks of settling back into the idea of *us* before Tank was done and moving my shit for me. Bossy asshole wouldn't have it any other way. I'm happy to be back in a place that feels like home though. This is where I want to be. This is where I want our baby to be. This is where I want my family to be.

Almost everything is ready for the baby. The room is ready, the crib's set up and bedding is in. The closet is full of tiny baby clothes, drawers are filled with diapers, creams, and wipes. Car seat is in my Jeep. Tank had a fucking fit when he found out they don't make car seats for bikes. Standing at the store, I was almost positive he was going to kill the pimply punk helping us. We got him one for the truck, but he's not happy about having to drive his truck if he's got the baby. Either way, we're ready; Just waiting for baby.

****

I'm so fucking sick of this shit. Jesus Christ.

"Tank!" I'm not sure how much more of this I can take. My back hurts. My legs are now chubby and wobbly and my ankles are swollen. The only thing that's stayed the same are my arms and face. I lean forward again, but I don't get anywhere.

"Fuck it." I give up. I can't paint my toenails and I hate it. It's probably a good thing I can't see my sausage toes now anyway. They'd probably make me cry.

"What?" Sticking his head around the door, he looks at me and smiles. Fuck him.

Throwing the bottle of pink nail polish at him, he catches it and laughs at me.

"Issues babe?" He damn well knows what my *issue* is.

Reaching a hand out, I just tell him, "Help my ass up."

"You want me to paint 'em, yeah?" He's going to paint my toenails?

"You're fuckin' with me, right?" Shaking his head he takes a few steps toward me and crouches down in front of me.

Smacking my thigh hard he grunts, "Foot." Putting my foot on his knee he smirks.

"What the fuck you grinnin' about." Shaking his head, he wipes that look off of his face. He can't fucking smirk at me like that and not explain. "What Tank?"

"Fat ass toes baby." Jerking my foot away I give him a nasty glare.

"You're an asshole."

"Know this baby. Now give me those fat feet."

19

Neanderthal

Tank

So I've gone through it all. The denial, the guilt, the fear, the shock, and all that other shit. Lil's a fucking badass, that's for fucking sure. Walking around with that baby kicking the living shit out her and still smiling, and still letting me fuck her. Shit is changing for her. Her body, her fucking mood, and her life. She's handling it like a pro. Me? Well shit's cool now. After I went through that shit show, things are relaxed now. I've got my woman back, my baby on the way, and my fucking club and brothers.

I'm here now ...

The fifth emotion is *Relaxation*. That's where I was a few weeks ago. Shit, I'm still kinda here now. This is when you're no longer stressed, because that baby isn't a tangible thing yet. To you it's just a thing we talk about, a thing your girl talks about all the damn time with every female within ear shot. It's just some clothes with tags on em', hanging on tiny ass hangers. Diapers and creams. Something we spend an ass ton of money on in every store we set foot in. It's just some bottles in the cupboard that I knock over every time I reach for a fucking cup. Maybe a crib in the spare room. This baby is just an idea right now. Right now the baby isn't real, because you can't see it or literally touch it. At this point in time, things are pretty good. You're coasting and things are smooth. Your girl's tits are getting bigger, and that body's looking hot as fuck, and now she's into fucking all the damn time like a dude. Shit is good.

The sixth and final emotion is something I can't really put into words. There's nothing that comes close to describing a feeling that strong. This thing, this baby, is completely amazing. It blows my mind every time I think about it. Never in my life have I encountered anything like it. It's your love for your girl times a million. Best fucking thing life has to offer.

****

It happened late one night a month back. Shit just caught me off guard and blew me away. Lil and me were lying on the couch, both laying sideways with Lil's back lying against my front. One of my arms were under her head, the other thrown over her stomach and our legs tangled. At this point, her belly had gotten bigger. She's not huge in my opinion. It's big enough for me to touch without her wanting to hit me every time. At this stage she's no longer saying she's just fat, thank fuck. That stage was terrible.

Since I've seen and explored every square inch of that perfect fucking body, I noticed that belly. And let me tell you, before Lil, I'd never thought about a pregnant bitch. I never spared them a second glance or thought. They didn't turn me on, but they did scare me. It's not that I was disgusted by them, I guess I just couldn't have cared less either way. Pregnancy happened to other people, not this motherfucker.

Now Lil being pregnant is something to see. Fuck, is she perfect. Hot as hell. Not a lot has changed on her. Her tits have gotten even bigger, which I sure as fuck enjoy, and her ass and hips have rounded out some. It's all fucking good, but it's that little belly. I fucking love that shit. Some strange sick Neanderthal thrill overcomes me every time I see it, every time I touch it. I swear it makes me want to tell everyone that I put that shit there. That's all me, all mine. That belly says more than any certificate, tattoo, ring, or cut ever could. That shit means that that girl is mine. That's my girl and my baby and I will kill anyone that comes close to fucking with that. Anyway, I'm off track. See Lil's bangin' body does that me.

Shit all changed for me the moment I felt it. Lil was asleep, out cold. My hand was lying over her stomach as I stared at the TV when I felt that little baby kick. Scariest, coolest, craziest, most emotional thing I've ever felt. I laid there for hours touching, poking, and pushing on her belly, just so I could feel it again. I was going to be a dad. Holy fuck, there's a baby in there and it's mine.

Then I got to see it. The day of her appointment, I got to see the second best thing that's ever happened to me.

We waited in the waiting room for the doctor. That was fucking torture. Nothin' but a bunch of big pregnant bitches staring at me while we wait. They were either eye fucking me or steering clear of me. Then there was the room. That room was scary all on its own. It would have been any male's idea of hell.

Pictures on the walls of various pussies and baby related posters closing in on me. Magazines and books dedicated to all things female and baby. The walls are some sickening bright pink and blue color. Girly chanting and moaning music playing through the room, making me twitchy. Fuck, on the table next to me was a board showing me just how much that baby will stretch my poor girl out. Some little shit in diapers was playing with a uterus. I wouldn't do this for any other bitch. Lil's lucky I love her so goddamn much.

"Miss Cruz." The little tart of a receptionist calls for Lil. I hate that shit. Hate that her last name isn't mine. That baby is coming with his or her parents having different last names and I hate it.

"That shit's changin' here real soon baby." I whisper loudly at her. She just waves me off and gives me an eye roll. I hope she knows that's a promise. I'm not fucking around. Blue eye shadow and red lipstick eye fucks me as we pass and if Lil catches that bitch looking at me, I can't be held accountable for what she does. She's pregnant and I let my baby do whatever the fuck she wants to. I'm not standing in her way. Showing us into a room, the bitch winks at me and closes the door.

Lil jumps up onto a table and starts pulling her clothes in all directions.

"The fuck ya doin'?" She looks at me with a wired expression. Before she can answer, a chubby little thing in a white lab coat waddles into the room.

"Good afternoon Lilly. How are you and that sweet little angel doing?" The doctor asks, touching Lil's stomach. I want to tell her to get the fuck away from my girl and my baby, but I know better. Lil would have my balls for it. Still I hate that shit, but fuck, what am I gonna do? Everyone does it and I've been learning to deal with it.

"We're good. How are you?" Lil smiles sweetly. There's that sweet ass Lil I don't get often.

"Wonderful. Let's get started."

The white lab coat lady proceeds to measure her stomach and then the bitch starts poking and pushing on my baby. I really want to fucking tell her to stop doing that shit but Lil gives me a glare once I open my mouth. Not sure why she's got to poke the fuck out of my girl and my baby, but what the fuck do I know?

"Would you mind getting the lights?" The doc asks me as she nods at the wall behind my head. Flipping the switch, the doctor pulls over a giant ass computer thing, kind of reminds me of the diagnostic we've got at the shop for the engines. Anyway, I'm stuck sitting here like an idiot, because I've got no fucking idea what's going on.

"Are you interested in finding the sex out today?" The doctor asks.

"Hell yeah!" I tell her.

"No!" Lil answers at the same time. "I wanna be surprised." Lil tells the doctor, but says it while staring me down with the devil in those eyes. Alright, I guess I'll shut the fuck up. The doc chuckles like that isn't the first time she's heard that shit.

"Alright, let's see what this little angel is doing in there ..." And that's when my life changed forever.

Some clear gel and that was it. A little black screen turned a fuzzy gray.

"Scoot up closer." The doc says, waving me over. Lil's staring at the screen. She doesn't even look at me when I sit by her. Doc starts moving that wand around and a strange as hell white, black, and gray mass shows up on the screen. Still not seeing shit. I've no idea what it is they're looking for because if this is what it is, then I'm lost.

"Not seein' shit." The doc laughs again. Lil doesn't even look at me.

"Lilly, could you turn your hips toward me a little." Lil shifts and the doctor starts to do her thing again. She moves around the wand and points to the screen and says, "There's a leg." That did not look like a leg. Jesus Christ, if that's the leg, then there is something wrong. It was a white line surrounded by black and gray. She's either really good at her job, because she can see that shit, or she's really bad, because I'm not seeing what she's seeing.

For ten minutes I stare at that screen, getting nothing. The doc takes pictures and rambles off info, percentiles, tests, sizes and shit.

"I've got you down for a three dimensional scan, correct?" The doc asks Lil.

"Yep."

The doc grins real big and says, "I love these." She fucking should. This shit cost me five hundred dollars. A few more buttons are pressed, and FINALLY, I fucking see it.

Craziest thing I've ever seen in my entire life. I can see the baby. Jesus Christ, it looks like a tiny ass human. I can see two arms. One is thrown out to the side and the other is curled into its side. Two perfect legs moving around and holy shit, there's a face. My baby has chubby ass cheeks, long eye lashes, and cute little lips. It even has hair.

"Holy fuck." Both Lil and the doctor turn their heads slowly to look at me. The doctor smiles and Lil's eyes are huge.

"Indeed. The baby looks really great. He or she weighs about seven pounds now and around eighteen inches. You've got a big, healthy baby there. Not too long now and you'll have him or her in your arms."

I can't look away. Scooting closer I can see fingers and toes. I can see every fucking thing. Fuck, I can see every perfect thing on my perfect little baby.

"That's my baby."

Life is fucking good. I wouldn't change this shit for anything.

20
Baby

Lil

Tank's four inches from the screen with his face practically pressed against it. He's all but blocked out my view now and I've given up trying to move him. He told me to shove over and that was it. Ten minutes ago the doctor told him she had other patients to see. He then proceeded to tell her he'd give her a thousand dollars to give us fifteen more minutes. My poor doctor is now printing off picture after picture and answering all kinds of crazy questions from my crazy ass man. It's kind of annoying because I have to pee so badly, but it's pretty fucking adorable too.

"Tank?" He doesn't even look at me. "Babe." I say shoving at his shoulder. He just shrugs me off. "Hello! Tank! Let's go."

"Shut it baby." I shut it and let him look at *his* baby, in his bossy way. *His* baby. We'll see whose baby it is at two in the morning when it's crying uncontrollably.

He got ten minutes more of that before I was done. I hopped up and left him staring at the screen like I just told him Santa is fake. Walking through the office, he's in baby land, staring at the pictures. Who knew such a bad ass would be so into something like this.

"Names?" He says out of nowhere.

"Excuse me?" What the hell is he rambling on about? I can't focus on anything other than the bathroom.

"Names for *my* baby, yeah?" Ah, so here we are. I have a feeling this is gonna be a battle.

"Do you have some picked out already?" I don't know why I'm even asking. Of fucking course he does. Bossy ass wouldn't have it any other way.

"Slash." He deadpans. I wait for the laugh to come out of him, but nothing. He's serious. Oh hell no. No fuckin' way.

"Seriously?"

"Thor?" Thor? Really? Did he really just suggest Thor to me? I just shake my head and head for the swinging door. I have no response for that.

"Harley or Trigger." He calls after me. I can't help it, I laugh. I laugh so damn hard I have to brace myself against the side of the building to keep from toppling over and cross my legs to keep from peeing myself, which did happen, just a little bit.

"You're joking, right?" I get out between my hysterical laughter.

"Fuck no." His arms are crossed over his chest and his brows are drawn together as he stares down at me with his mouth in an unamused hard line.

"For one. Those names? Not happenin', no matter how much you pout."

"Education. I don't fuckin' pout."

"Whatever you say. Those names though? No go. Never gonna happen so get them outta your thick head right now. Two, they're all boy names. There's a fifty percent chance it's a girl."

In my heart I could care less either way. It used to drive me bat shit crazy when you asked an expectant mother what sex she hoped her baby would be and she'd answer with that cliché response, "I don't care as long as it's healthy." It's true, I really don't care as long as my baby comes out healthy. But that tiny, bitchy biker brat in me rears her ugly head and says "Girl. Girl. Girl." Just to spite him. Shaking his head he grumbles and growls.

"No fuckin' girls. No. Not happenin'." Impossibly stubborn asshole.

"I'm havin' a girl just to drive you crazy."

We got to the club and Tank showed everyone the picture of *his* baby. He went on and on until even I was annoyed with him. He really is into this whole baby thing. It's kind of sweet that he's into this so goddamn much. Sitting on the couch now, I watch Tank talk to Leo, Tiny and Gin. The three of them are huddled by the bar in a big ol' biker circle. They're doing their typical grunt, nod, coded word conversation about God knows what. I find it funny that even inside, away from outside prying eyes and unfriendly ears, they still talk like this. I mean, I could give a fuck less about what they're talking about. Seriously, none of us Old Ladies care about their shit. If I really wanted to know, I could get him alone and fuck it out of him anyway. Give him some pussy and he'll be spilling all kinds of secrets. He'd be a shit spy.

"Watcha' talkin' 'bout, babe?" I've gotta fuck with him. It's to alluring not to. Tipping his head in my direction, he lifts an eyebrow while looking at me like I've lost my ever loving mind. "Don't worry 'bout it. Club shit babe." Club shit? Ya don't say.

"You talkin' 'bout that new line on the blow or the possible new brothers?" I don't even get a response. He just throws his hands in the air and stomps off grumbling, "Fuckin' mouthy ass woman. Not tellin' her shit again."

"Damn brother, stop tellin' your Old Lady all our business." Leo mumbles, shaking his head.

"Well there goes all our fuckin' secrets." Gin laughs and smiles at me. Men, I swear. They're worse than bitches.

But this is the Tank I've missed. This is man I've been waiting for. The one who is interested in his club again. The guy who holds down his club and his brothers. The one who is bossy and a huge asshole. The man who keeps me close. The Tank that loves me enough to keep me in the loop. I've missed this Tank. Finally I have him back. Even if he's grumbling and growling about me sticking my nose in club business, I still fucking love him.

****

"Doctor said I can still fuck you baby." He informs me while smashing me into the bed. His face is in my neck and his hand is twisted up in my hair, pulling on it.

"Keep layin' on me like that 'n you're gonna squish the baby right out of me." Groaning he rolls off me and onto this back, right next to me. Throwing an arm over his head, he grumbles.

"Killed the fuckin' mood Lil! Talkin' 'bout squeezin' a baby out of your pussy. Freaks me the fuck out."

"Just wait 'till I push one out." He grumbles and groans. Hopping up, he shakes his head.

"You're a mean fuckin' woman, ya know that?" He growls waving around a hand at his hard dick. I just laugh. "Fuckin' tease me in the hall then ya start talkin' baby. Jesus Christ." He stomps his way into the bathroom. The shower starts and he says, "You're an asshole Lilly."

"But you still love me."

"Baby yeah, I fuckin' do. But you're still a goddamn pain in my ass."

He damn near fucked that baby right out of me. That night our lives changed forever.

****

Ty Trace. That's my son's name. My *Son*. I have a son. It's insane. He's so small and so perfect. He has Tanks dark hair, his lips, his nose, his jaw. They're goddamn twins, and he's so perfect. I've never seen anything like him. It's hard not to cry when I look at him. From the moment he took his first breath, I knew I'd love him until I took my last.

Seven hours of hard labor. Crying, squeezing Tanks hand, yelling at everyone, hitting Tank, and throwing out every dirty word known to man, and it happened so fast after that. The doctor said, "It's a boy" and that was it for us. I've never seen Tank cry, but there were tears. Not many, but they were there.

"Here mommy." The doctor said, handing me my son. God I have a son that looks exactly like his dad and it's terrifying.

"Give him to Tank." The doctor, nurses, Tank, and everyone there all looked at me like I was fucking nuts. "I've had nine months with him. I have the rest of my life to hold him. Give him to Tank."

"Baby, I don't know." He's scared. I've never seen this kind of scared from him before. His hands are shaking and his eyes are huge.

"You'll be great." I encourage him, even though I've got to admit … I'm a little nervous handing over *my son*. He's been only mine for nine long months, and now it's time to trust someone else with him. Tank would never hurt our son, but he's just so small and fragile. The doctor hands him to Tank.

"He's tiny. You lied doc. Ya said he was gonna be big."

She laughs and shakes her head. "Nine pounds is big. He's big and healthy. You two will be fine."

Sitting down in the reclining chair in our room, he looks down at the baby and starts talking to him.

"Doc says we'll be *fine,* so don't hold it against me if I man handle ya a little bit, buddy. I'm new at this shit." Ty just wiggles around a little and yawns. Unwrapping Ty, I watch Tank poke and prod at him.

"What are you doing?"

"Don't worry 'bout it baby. Just get some damn sleep."

"Bossy ass."

"Mommy thinks I'm bossy, but mommy's wrong. She's the bossy one. Not too long now n' it'll be you she'll be bossin'. Sorry to say bud, but it's gonna be like that the rest of your damn life."

"Don't tell him that," I yawn. I'm tired. Giving birth is exhausting. Tanks got him so I figure ten quick minutes of rest will be okay. Closing my eyes, I catch Tank lifting Ty up and laying him on his chest, propping his own feet up as he leans back.

"You're my son. You're a damn Tank, buddy."

****

Ty's a week old and I've held him maybe nine times since we brought him home. Okay so that's an exaggeration, but it fucking feels like it. If Tank's not hogging him, it's someone else. Gin's always hovering, trying to steal him from whoever has him. Peaches insists on putting every article of clothing he owns on him. Mary and Kiki are always smudging his face with red lipped kisses, and Cali has to cuddle him any time she sees him. Stitch *shows* him the bikes. Happy warns him off women, and Rampage will only hold him if he's asleep, because according to him, that's the only time he's not crying.

The guys hold him and tell him all the ridiculous shit they're going to let him do as soon as he's walking. The Old Ladies "ooh" and "aah" him constantly. My son will always have a family, because everyone loves that little baby.

I took him to see my dad and he fell in love instantly. Hell, he was even able to pull some strings and get a visit where he could hold him. God it was hard to see him hold Ty and not be able to come home with us so he could see him daily, but he got to touch him and Ty held his finger. It was perfect. I just hope and pray he can beat this shit and come home to his family soon. Ty needs him. I need him. His family needs him.

****

"You guys are takin' up the entire bed." Tank is lying in bed with Ty on his chest. This is how it's been since we've brought him home. A king size bed and I get a foot of it. Tanks watching TV and playing with *his* Ty's tiny fingers. Looking at him holding our son makes me fall in love all over again. He's so gentle with him. I didn't know what to expect, but he's an amazing Dad.

"Too bad babe." Looking down at Ty he says, "Mommy's ridin' couch tonight." For fucks sake. For such a big ass, mean man, he sure is cuddly with that baby.

"You're lucky you're holdin' the baby." I warn him. Tank just laughs that deep gruff laugh. He scoots over and nods me over.

"You're lucky I love you so fuckin' much."

Looking down at Ty he says, "We love mommy, so I guess we can let her sleep with us." Crawling in bed with Tank and Ty, I lean my head onto Tanks shoulder. This is where I want to be. This where I've always wanted to be.

Kissing his shoulder I tell him, "I love you."

"Baby, yeah. I know you do."

Epilogue

Five years later. ...

Tank

"Babe!" I stick my head out the door and yell. Yeah I'm feeling that crazy panic shit work its way up. Where the fuck did she go now? Told her we had ten minutes, then I was leaving her the fuck here. If she doesn't get her ass in here real quick, I might lose it. I'm trying not to flip my shit here. Count to ten asshole. Yeah, fuck that counting.

"Lilly!" I stick my head out the door and yell again. Gin's just standing in the hall, leaning against the wall laughing at me. Fucking asshole, this shit isn't funny. Rampage took one look inside the bathroom and turned on his heel, and high tailed his ass right out of here. I don't blame him.

"God dammit. LIL! Get the fuck in here"

"What the hell?" She sputters as she comes to a stop in front of the bathroom door. Her eyes are huge and her face is stricken with panic. For a second I'm distracted. Goddamn, she looks fucking hot. A long white dress with no straps and her tits are about to fall out of it. I could rip that fucker right off her and fuck her right here. I like that idea a whole fuck of a lot.

Her hair is a mess of curls on her head, and I wanna wrap my hands up in it and pull on it. Bare feet, pink toes and all. My dick twitches in my jeans and my balls start to ache.

"Tank!" She snaps at me. Right, I was about to go crazy. Fuck! Lil's body does that shit to me. I start forgetting shit.

"What the fuck she doin'?" I ask Lil, because I have no fucking clue. And this shit is scary as fuck to me so I'm not even sure how to approach it.

Lil's mouth gapes at me and her eye brow raises in suspicion. Oh fuck me, there's the devil in those eyes.

"Seriously? You were screamin' for me over this?" She mutters as she waves a hand toward the cute little shit sitting on my bathroom counter, looking proud as fuck with her little paint job. Of course Lil doesn't care. Hell, she looks proud too. She probably started this shit. Just fucking shoot me now. Put one right between my goddamn eyes. If this is how it's going to be, just put me out of my motherfucking misery.

"I sure the fuck am serious. Why the fuck she paintin' that shit on her goddamn face baby?" Throwing her hands in the air, Lil shakes her head and ignores me. With an annoyed grumble, she yells over her shoulder.

"Because she's a little fuckin' girl, Tank."

Holy fucking shit. Not a good enough reason. Not even close to a good enough reason. This is not happening. Gin and I both stand here for a minute, still trying to come up with something.

Finally, Gin just shakes his head and shrugs. "Man, that little girl is gonna kill me too." Gin grumbles as he walks off. Fuck yeah, I'm right there with ya brother.

My baby is supposed to stay a baby. Where's my tiny little thing? Where is my baby with those dark curls, rosy cheeks, and doe eyes? Looking at her now, I can't handle this shit. Her little chubby hands are clutching a doll as she stares in the mirror and smiles at herself.

My daughter is not starting this shit already. She's gonna stay my baby. Jesus fucking Christ, she's two. Two years old, she is still my baby.

"Dada, me pitty wike mama." Those big ol' brown eyes and pig tails say from the bathroom counter, holding a stick of something red in her free hand. Lil's makeup is spilled out everywhere and smeared on every square inch of my bathroom. My baby has lipstick all over the place and black shit all around her eyes.

"You're two." I tell her simply, because what the fuck am I going to say to her? I'm sure the fuck not going to yell at my sweet baby. She gives me attitude with the mention of her being two. There's her mama right there. Those chubby hands are on her sides and the devil in her big brown eyes.

"No Dada. Me big wike mama now." Lord help me. I can't handle this shit. Kill me, just fucking kill me. I was made for boys, not little girls.

"Lil. Get your ass in there n' take that shit off my baby before I lose my shit."

****

Standing outside with my brothers, we watch my second miracle run around the club backyard with Gin's little shit headed boy. They're throwing rocks at each other, being boys. No matter how many times you tell 'em to knock their shit off, they still do it. Fuck it, they put an eye out, it's on them. Owen, Gin's son is three. Ty, my boy, is turning five. Ty is one of the best things besides Lil and my baby girl that has ever happened to me. I can't imagine life without them. Looking at him, it hits me how much time flies. I try not to miss shit, but still, I feel like time's passing too goddamn fast. He's getting so fuckin big and smart now.

"Dad! You see me hit Owen with that rock?" Boys, now this is shit I can handle.

The third best thing that ever happened to me comes running outside, pig tails bouncing and chubby legs going sans makeup a few minutes later.

"Dada!"

I don't know what's scarier, the fact the she looks exactly like Lil, or the fact that she acts just like her. Not sure I'll make it to her eighteenth birthday with her looking like Lil. She's already got me and the guys antsy and twitchy about how to handle what she's gonna bring in the future.

She reaches for me, but punks me at the last second and dodges around me, going right for Stitch instead when he mentions candy.

"Let's eat lots of candy, baby." Stitch says to her, but looks right at me.

"Fuck you." He just laughs.

My baby just waves at me and smiles at Stitch. He thinks he won her love, but too fucking bad. She'll love anyone of these motherfuckers as long as they give her candy.

I thought Lil had my heart, but looking at my baby, I not so sure anymore. It's a fucking tossup. My baby came at three in the damn morning on a day where we'd seen the worst snow storm in decades. Drama just like her mama. Of course Lil couldn't wait to give birth until during the day. No, it had to be the middle of the fucking night, four degrees below zero, and a fucking foot of snow. It was a day that Gin, Stitch, Rampage, me and Ty had spent five hours, neck deep in Christmas shit and snow, putting up decorations like my bossy ass women told me to do. That miracle

came wrapped up in a pink blanket, wailing and making a fuss,

weighing in at six pounds, four ounces and nineteen and a half

inches long a few hours later. A dark mess of curls, soft skin, and

big, deep brown eyes. Rowan looked exactly like her mama;

Perfect. Never saw something so perfect. My son is pretty fucking

perfect too. I'm pretty goddamn lucky.

My boy looks just like me. He came weighing in at nine

pounds, one ounce. He's big as fuck now too. The only thing that

boy got from his mamma are her eyes. That little girl is all her

mama's though. Fucking perfection. No fucking idea how I helped

create two things so completely amazing, but somehow I did.

Although I'm still saying it was all Lil. That woman is capable of

preforming fucking miracles, that's for goddamn sure.

"Her face better now, asshole?" Lil asks me as she leans

into my side. Much fucking better.

"Shit yeah. She's too young for that shit babe."

Rolling her eyes she says, "You're gonna be so much fun when she's a teenager." I know I will, but Lil will put up with my ass. She always does. The only woman on this goddamn earth that would love me after all the shit I threw at her over the years. Stuck by my side through it all. No matter how bad shit got, she was right there. There was a time I never thought I'd get here and if I did, I wasn't sure Lil would be here with me. I thank fuck every day I'm here with her. I'm one lucky motherfucker.

It's crazy how much I love that woman. Not a goddamn thing I did to deserve her or my kids, but I'm fucking thankful for them every day. This is a life I never imagined for myself. A life I never thought I wanted until I had it. Lil and my kids are something I'd die for. They're something I wouldn't give up for anything.

****

The fire's blazing, food's on the grill, and drinks are in the ice chest as Lil leans into me, her back leaning against my front.

Kids are runnin' around being shits like usual, my brothers and their families are here. Life has changed in the past few years, but shit is still good. Shit is exactly how I want it.

Tags and Low are by the grill flipping all kinds of meat, when Low holds up the spatula and waves me over with it. Low, now there's a motherfucker I wasn't sure I'd ever see on the outside again. He was acquitted six months ago. He served five and a half years for a shit ton of other charges, but they dropped the murder charge due to lack of evidence. Lil's so goddamn happy to have him back. He officially stepped down as President, and I was voted in. Said to me he just wanted to be a grandpa and a member. I'm okay with that shit, but don't get it twisted, that asshole still barks orders at everyone. Still, it's still good to have him back.

Tags is still looking for Miss right. He met a bitch, but something happened and he won't talk about it. Peaches was finally able to lock that asshole Gin down, got married and they had Owen.

Leo is still at the bar talking nonsense, while Mary is right there with him. Tiny is still avoiding the whores and Kiki is still bitching at him for it. Happy's still not the same, but he's been getting there. It's been a long time, but since the kids came into our lives, he's been slowly coming out of his shell, which is a good thing 'cause Lil has missed him. She still loves the shit out of his grouchy ass.

Stitch and Cali, well there's a story for another time. Arms and Melli are working on building their own army. Four kids now. I swear, these past few years Melli's been knocked up the entire time. They seem so damn happy, so it's all good. Rampage met his match in Lil's friend Lailah, but shit was a struggle for them. He fucking loves the fuck outta that girl, even if he won't say it. Don't know how she puts up with him, but I'm happy for him.

Sargent, Crush, King, Blade, and Kash are still a bunch of single assholes. Life's fucking good. Took a long time to get here, but shit is perfect.

"Foods done." Peaches yells at Lil, waving us over. Lil slides her hand down my arm and entwines those little fingers around mine. I can feel her all the way to my bones. I'll always know her touch. Not a goddamn thing has changed. She's still the reason I get out of bed, and still the reason I live life. Her hand in mine brings shit right back. For a moment I'm pulled right back to six years ago in this same fucking spot.

Free Bird is playing through the air. The family is hanging around, talking and laughing with one another. Her hands are on her hips, those big doe eyes blinking up at me through thick, dark lashes as she stares at me like I'm the best motherfucking thing she's ever seen. And so much power. A power I now know she holds over me. A power I'd gladly give up to her and my mind goes back to this same moment, six years ago when she came to me.

"Dance with me," she says. It's not a question. Girl just demands and I follow. There's nothing I wouldn't do for the look on her face right now. That happy content smile has me.

"Yeah babe," I agree without question.

I'm fucking lucky she's my family. I'm just so fucking lucky she's mine. So fucking lucky she loves me. I couldn't imagine myself without her. I couldn't *see* anything without her. She's it for me.

"I love you, Tank."

"Baby, yeah. I fuckin' love you too."

42649846R00173

Made in the USA
Lexington, KY
30 June 2015